MW01242939

WHISLING ISLAND MIRACLES

A WHISLING ISLAND NOVEL

JULIA CLEMENS

PICKLED PLUM PUBLISHING

CHAPTER ONE

NORA TOOK Mack's hand in hers as they walked along the circular driveway toward Bobby's new home on Whisling. He'd closed on the sale a few months before, but this was the first time Nora was seeing the home. And it was massive.

Not that she'd expect anything less. He was Bobby, after all. The man liked to make a statement with everything he did. But this mega-mansion seemed a little extreme, even for the guy who'd bought Nora diamond earrings for their one-month anniversary . . . as a *teenager*.

"It's nice," Mack said brightly. A little too brightly.

Mack had promised to get along with Bobby for the sake of their new family. He'd quickly realized that loving Nora meant loving Amber, which had been easy for him. But loving Amber meant accepting Bobby. That part hadn't been as simple, but in the past few months, Mack had made progress. So much progress that Nora only felt the slightest bit of hesitation bringing him along to a family dinner.

Tonight, they'd come at Amber's request. Her parents were in town, and she really wanted a nice sit-down dinner with all her family on the island: Nora, her birth mom; Bobby, her birth dad; Tabby and Gerry, her parents; Mack, Nora's boyfriend; and of course Elise, her sister.

It was quite the crowd, so during the planning, Bobby had offered his home as a meeting place instead of one of the restaurants on the island. Amber had jumped at the opportunity. She'd felt a home would create just the atmosphere she was hoping for.

After the venue for the dinner had been announced, Nora had immediately felt anxious. But it wasn't like she could offer her nine-hundred square foot condo as an alternative. She reminded herself this was about Amber, not her or Mack.

And that's how Nora wound up on the doorstep of her ex-boyfriend's home with her current boyfriend, about to have dinner with the people who'd raised the daughter she'd given up for adoption when she was just a teen. Yes, Nora had a strange life. But it was more than she could've dreamed of, even a year before, so she was going to shut up and be grateful.

Mack, feeling the nervous energy emanating from Nora, was working hard to be the support system she needed. He held her hand tightly and kept his opinions of Bobby to himself (Bobby had made a terrible first impression on Mack, flirting with Nora and then accusing Mack of upsetting her). If Mack could pull off this sweet demeanor all evening, he deserved a medal.

The door opened before Nora could ring the bell. She was surprised to see Bobby, not a butler dressed in a tux, on the other side of the door.

Bobby looked nice in his green button up, which was hanging untucked over his khaki chinos. Bare feet completed his look, giving Nora the go-ahead to kick off her heels the second she walked in the door. The two-story-high atrium they walked into wasn't exactly the kind of entry one left their shoes at, but if Bobby was going shoe-free, Nora would as well. The fitted, little white dress she wore was restricting enough. She wasn't going to add heels to the mix any longer than she had to.

"Leave them by the statue," Bobby offered as he nodded toward a marble statue of a waterfall in the middle of the atrium. Again, over-the-top, but somehow it worked.

Nora nudged her shoes with her foot to the base of the statue, and Mack took his designer loafers off as well. Nora knew that was a huge concession; Mack loved his shoes. But he was showing he was part of the group. The shoeless group? It was weird, but Nora felt like it was a move in the right direction.

Unlike Bobby, Mack's baby blue button up was tucked into his navy blue dress pants, showing off his trim waist and broad shoulders. Bobby wasn't bad looking—he'd aged well—but he just couldn't compare to the man by her side. Mack's mahogany-colored hair had grown out in the last couple of months, and his luxurious mane fell effortlessly, looking mussed and yet put together all at the same time. Between Mack's physique, his hair, and his deep blue eyes, he was more of a work of art than the beautiful statue in Bobby's atrium. And although it certainly didn't hurt that he was so nice to look at, those good looks were way far down on the list of things that made him the perfect man for Nora.

"Amber and Elise will be here with Gerry and Tabby soon. Apparently, their flight out of Kansas City was delayed for a couple of hours, so they only arrived in Seattle about two hours ago. But they got to the ferry terminal quickly and will be here in about fifteen minutes or so," Bobby explained as he led Nora and Mack into his kitchen.

On the massive Carrera marble island that sat in the middle of the room were laid hors d'oeuvres of all sorts. Nora would've loved to dig in if it weren't for what Bobby had said. No one else was there? She'd been sure that showing up ten minutes late would've given Amber and Elise enough time to arrive first. But they weren't there? Meaning she and Mack were Bobby's only guests? The thought made her nervous.

"Oh, that's too bad for Gerry and Tabby. But I'm glad the flight wasn't cancelled," Mack said as he led Nora to the island full of food and then nodded toward the plates. Thankfully, her boyfriend wasn't at a loss for words like she was.

"Me too," Bobby agreed with a nod before motioning toward the food Nora had been staring at. "Feel free to dig in. The caterer set these up. She'll be back in half an hour to serve our meal."

A caterer. At a small, casual family dinner.

Nora breathed in through her nose. This was what having a child with Bobby was like. One reason that Nora was grateful she'd given Amber up for adoption was that they'd been able to avoid all this pomp and grandeur for Amber's entire childhood. Nora hated it, and she was sure Amber would've been a completely different woman had this been her normal. Besides, Nora couldn't have raised her on her own as well as Tabby and Gerry had, and now Amber had two sets of parents and families who loved and adored her.

This meal with Bobby would be overwhelming enough, but Nora thought back to when she was just a teen and Amber had turned one. Had she and Bobby been the ones to try to raise Amber, what would that party have been like? Suddenly, visions of elaborate gatherings and over-the-top events, followed by nights alone with Amber while Bobby went out and did who knew what came to Nora's mind. It was all too easy to imagine the path not traveled. Nora was grateful that she'd made the decision she had—even if it had torn her in two all those years ago—because it had been best for all of them, especially Amber.

"Thank you," Nora managed as she took a small glass plate and placed a caviar covered cracker and a gorgeous piece of shrimp onto her plate.

Wait, was the plate crystal? Nora was tempted to dump off her food to check, but decorum won out. Still, she was pretty sure the plate was crystal.

From the kitchen, there were two steps that took them down into a living space. Nora was sure it had to be one of many, considering the size of the home. A lavishly large, light blue sectional couch framed the space, and the floor to ceiling doors were opened all the way so that, even in the kitchen, it felt they were practically standing on the beach. Between the crystal plates, the statue, and the view, it all felt like too much to Nora. It was not at all what she was used to.

"You have a beautiful home." Mack kept the conversation going, even though he had every right not to. He and Bobby weren't friends. Nora should've been the one to bridge the gap. But because she wasn't doing it, Mack was stepping up. He was better than she deserved. But she wasn't about to point that out to him.

"Thank you. I got lucky with my timing. It actually belonged to a friend of a friend who decided that since she's retiring, she'd rather have a vacation home in Bora Bora. Our mutual friend mentioned I was looking for a home here, and it happened pretty fast," Bobby said as he followed Mack down the line of food, filling his own plate with the tiny appetizers.

"It was fast," Nora said, the opulence feeling a little less overwhelming now that they were eating and talking. She could do this. She would do this.

She wasn't sure why the appearance of Bobby's home had hit her so hard. It wasn't any more than she'd imagined—the house he'd lived in when Nora had been dating him was actually even bigger than this one. Maybe it was because now she realized this could've been her life. If she'd gone to Bobby instead of following the advice of those who had been around her, Nora knew without a doubt Bobby would have provided for her. For them. But in this way. A way she would have never been comfortable living.

Her reaction today wasn't at all one of feeling inadequate or wondering *what if*. It was the opposite, in fact. She was grateful she was right where she was. And she couldn't be more impressed with who Amber was and what she'd accomplished in her short life. Which was shocking to her. She never expected to one day be so at peace with her decision from over twenty-five years ago.

Now that her thoughts were sorted, she really needed to focus on this conversation. Help Mack out a bit.

"I could tell you thought so from your reaction during our dinner with Amber," Bobby said, his voice light with teasing.

"I wasn't that bad," Nora defended.

"Your face looked like this," Bobby said before dropping his mouth open and widening his eyes.

Nora shook her head, but Mack began to laugh. "You do that impression really well," he said through his laughter.

Nora nudged Mack in the ribs with her elbow, but not too hard considering this was exactly what she wanted. All of them engaging in conversation, even laughter, together. Although it was at her expense.

The doorbell chimed a song through the home, saving Nora from any more teasing for the time being.

Bobby left the kitchen and soon came back followed by Gerry, Tabby, Amber, and Elise.

"Sounds like it was a rough travel day," Nora said as she moved in to hug Tabby.

Who would have thought Nora would gain a friend who felt more like a sister when she'd started her search for her daughter?

"Oh boy, was it. But we're here now," Tabby said as she returned Nora's embrace enthusiastically.

"Our airport has one of Gerry's favorite burger places though, so he was kind of in heaven," Tabby added as she pulled away from Nora and moved to shake Mack's hand in greeting.

"I let myself get a burger each time our flight was delayed. It was a game where I was the winner either way," Gerry said with a smile as he shook Nora's hand, and all the greetings were complete.

The girls stood in a corner of the kitchen as they watched the exchange, a wide grin on both their faces. Nora met Elise's eye, and the sweet girl winked. Nora could've never guessed that she'd gain a bonus family when she'd made that heart-wrenching decision all those years ago. But Elise was now as precious to her as Amber.

"I'm guessing you aren't up for hors d'oeuvres, then?" Bobby asked, motioning to the overflowing island.

"Gerry may have eaten three burgers, but I'm starving," Tabby said, not waiting for another invitation. Soon her crystal plate was full of food. She moved to stand next to Nora as she tried a puffed pastry.

"These are amazing," she moaned as soon as her mouth was clear of food.

"I'll pass your compliments along to the chef," Bobby said with a proud smile.

"Oh, let me try," Elise said, getting her own plate, and Amber followed suit.

"Are these plates crystal?" Elise asked, flipping the plate before she put any food on it.

Bobby shrugged. "Maybe? My assistant bought all the stuff for this place. He just knows what I like and then sends me the bill when all's said and done."

"Maybe we need your assistant to come work for us. These are exquisite," Elise said as she admired the plate.

Amber nodded as she looked around at the rest of the home. "And look at those couches," she added.

Elise murmured her agreement.

"I love you girls a whole lot, but even for you two, I couldn't give up Trey," Bobby said with a shrug of his shoulders.

Amber laughed and Elise fake pouted. "What if we asked really nicely?" she pushed.

"I'd say *thank you for asking so nicely, but no*," Bobby replied.

This time the entire group laughed and then fell into small conversations around the kitchen. The girls moved closer to Bobby, asking questions about his new home. As far as Nora knew, the girls hadn't been here either. Bobby had been hoping to spend more time on Whisling these past couple of months, but work hadn't allowed it. This was his first full weekend on the island since buying his house. He'd come up from LA a couple of times before, but it had only been for specific events for the girls and he always had to fly out immediately afterward.

Gerry and Mack began a conversation about the draft. Apparently, Gerry wasn't happy about the picks his team had made, but Mack was thrilled about his.

Tabby pulled Nora to the side. "Have you figured out the reason behind this dinner?" Tabby whispered before popping another of the pastries into her mouth.

Nora shook her head.

"Don't you think it's odd? Amber has only ever asked us to fly out for business reasons. But this feels personal, doesn't it?" Tabby asked.

Nora hadn't even thought twice about them all getting together. Probably because she hadn't known Amber had asked her parents to fly out. Nora had assumed Gerry and Tabby were coming into town, thus the reason for this dinner: so the seven of them could spend time together while Bobby was on Whisling.

But with the new information Tabby had just offered, Nora was now curious as well.

"Do you think they have some sort of announcement?" Tabby asked. "They've been talking about expanding their business to Seattle. Maybe it's about that?"

Nora shrugged. Tabby's guess would be better than hers. Tabby knew their girls much better than Nora did. Although, like Tabby, Nora had also heard Amber and Elise talking about hiring someone who could oversee the Seattle side of operations. They'd been saying that travel didn't always go smoothly between the city and the island, and having someone there to greet their guests and bring them to the ferry or helicopter would be helpful. That person could also work with investors who lived in the city. But so far they hadn't been able to find the right person they trusted enough to take on so much, considering how important all those relationships were to their business. So Tabby's guess felt right.

"What are you two whispering about?" Amber asked as she joined the women.

"Just wondering why you brought us all here." Tabby answered honestly.

"All in good time, Mama," Amber said with a light laugh as two women Nora hadn't seen before joined them in the kitchen. Both were wearing aprons that read *Little Sunshine Catering.*

"Oh, looks like dinner is ready," Bobby said, noticing the additions to the room as well.

"We can come back if this isn't a good time," a woman holding more trays of food said.

"It's perfect timing," Bobby said with his winning grin that had both women blushing. And there was that charm that had everyone loving Bobby but reminded Nora why she'd never been able to fully trust him. Charm, especially Bobby's charm, had a way of hiding a whole lot.

Bobby led them into the dining room that was just to the left of the living room. The table sat perpendicular to the floor to ceiling window so that everyone could have a nearly perfect view of the ocean just outside the home. The room was lit with the pinks and oranges of the sunset. Much of Bobby's house was too much, but this part suited Nora just right.

Salad plates and bowls of homemade rolls hit the table just after they were all seated. Little Sunshine Catering didn't mess around.

"Okay, will you tell us all now?" Elise asked as soon as Amber had dug into her salad.

Amber covered her mouth when a laugh tried to escape her. "There's that patience you're so famous for," Amber teased her sister.

"Wait, Elise isn't in on this?" Tabby asked since her guess of why they were there had just gone out the window.

Mack and Gerry had taken seats closest to the window. Nora sat beside Mack and Tabby beside her husband. Elise was at Nora's left while Amber had taken the seat beside her mom. Bobby had filled the spot at the head of the table.

It was because of Nora's proximity to Elise that she noticed the way the girl stiffened at Tabby's words. Nora immediately picked up on the fact that Elise wasn't happy about being kept in the dark; she was just trying to appear at ease. So Nora decided not to ask Elise if she was doing alright. Elise seemed to want to ignore any ill feelings she was having in that moment.

"I wanted to tell you all at once," Amber said, her fingers drumming against the table, her salad all but abandoned. "And I can soon."

The doorbell rang.

"Oh, I guess I can now," Amber said as she stood and hurried to the front door before Bobby could beat her to it.

"I knew it," Elise muttered, the tension in her shoulders easing.

That was a good sign.

Nora felt less anxious as well, until Amber returned with the chef from their lodge. Why would Amber have brought Raul to a family dinner? Unless . . . Nora's thoughts began to run wild until Amber's voice put them on hold.

"Um," Amber began nervously, looking up at the man who had an arm around her waist. A very comfortable looking arm. As if he'd stood just like this with Amber many times before.

Nora took in the man before her. The man who looked like he belonged next to her daughter. He was handsome; there was no getting around that. With his square jaw and his midnight black hair, he was debonair personified, if not a little hard looking. It didn't help that his shirt barely contained a massively muscled chest, arms, shoulders. But then he smiled down at Amber and a light filled him, softening every part of his face. Amber seemed to melt with that smile, and she turned confidently to her family.

"You might be wondering why Raul is here," Amber said, taking in the crowd.

Tabby and Gerry were turned in their seats so that they could see the pair. From what Nora could see, it looked like Tabby wore a smile, but Gerry's face showed nothing—as if he was waiting to see what happened before conveying any emotion. Bobby leaned forward on his elbows as he examined the pair while Mack leaned back in his seat, his arms crossed over his chest. Both men wore the same expression as Gerry.

Elise watched the pair curiously. As if she'd suspected something but it was the first time seeing them interact like this. Which was surprising, considering Elise worked and lived with Amber. So it had to be a new development.

But Amber's sister didn't smile. Did that mean she didn't

approve? And because she knew Raul best out of the people in the room, besides Amber, Nora valued her opinion. But then again, four out of the six of them weren't smiling. Nora felt she had to even those odds a bit. So she smiled at the still-nervous looking pair.

"We are," Gerry finally answered for the group.

"I thought it would be best. I mean, *we* thought it would be best . . ." Amber amended as she looked at Raul. "We wanted to tell you, the most important people in my life, first. All together."

Amber's face was splotchy, somehow red with embarrassment but a little pale at the same time.

"They'll be happy for us," Raul whispered, but the room was so quiet that everyone heard him.

Amber nodded as she took in a deep breath.

Elise watched her sister closely as Amber spoke again. "We wanted to tell you all that Raul and I are . . ." Amber began, pausing again to look up at Raul.

He gave her a reassuring nod.

As Amber opened her mouth to speak, Elise muttered, "Dating," fully expecting to speak the same word as her sister as Amber said, "Getting married."

"What?!" Elise yelped. She seemed to be the first to digest the news.

Nora looked at every face at the table, each displaying complete shock.

Amber was doing the same thing as Nora, wringing her hands as she took in each expression.

"I wouldn't have brought mom and dad out here just to tell them I was dating a new guy," Amber said, trying to show the group reason.

Nora guessed that was true.

Wait, had Amber really said *getting married*? To Raul? When had this happened?

"I would have also thought that you would date a guy before marrying him," Elise countered.

Nora thought that was true as well.

"I did date Raul," Amber countered.

"Secretly?" Elise asked, her hurt evident with just that one word.

"Technically, he works for us, so it all felt too messy. We thought it would be best to keep it between the two of us until we were more serious."

"Well, you sure as heck are serious now," Elise muttered, shaking her head in disbelief.

"Give your sister some more time to explain," Gerry said, entering the conversation.

"Fine," Elise said, crossing her arms. "Explain."

"You knew I thought Raul was cute."

"Cute and getting married are worlds apart. Universes," Elise said before Gerry sent her a warning look.

Elise snapped her lips shut and looked at her sister.

"We started working together closely for the grand opening and both knew the other was interested. He finally asked me out the day after."

"You've been dating him since the grand opening? And you told me nothing?!"

Gerry's next warning look went unseen by his distraught daughter.

Nora sat stone still, unsure of how to react to all of this.

"It was weird," Amber pleaded, trying to get Elise to understand.

"All the more reason to tell me," Elise countered.

Amber moved closer to Raul, as if she needed his strength.

"You would have told me all the reasons why I shouldn't date our chef," Amber returned.

"How do you know? You never gave me the chance," Elise said as her eyes dropped to the table.

Amber looked pleadingly at Tabby.

"Elise," Tabby began.

"Are you going to take her side?" Elise asked, her eyes shooting up to look at her mom before Tabby could say anything more.

"I don't think that there are sides here," Tabby replied softly.

"According to Amber there are. There's her and Raul on one side and then me, the one who would've been against them. Although I was never even given the chance to approve or disapprove. I was tried and found lacking, all while being ignorant to everything," Elise retorted.

"I'm telling you now," Amber said, holding her hand out toward her sister.

"You're telling us *all* now. Big difference, Ber."

"You're my family. I wanted to tell you guys together. I didn't want to make you keep a secret," Amber tried to explain.

"When has that ever kept you from telling me anything before?" Elise asked, her voice nearing squeaky range.

Amber's eyes dropped as tears began to stream down her face.

Nora ached to take Amber in her arms, and even as she thought the words, Raul did just that.

With Amber cared for, Nora looked to her side to see matching tears on Elise's cheeks.

Tabby ran around the table to hug Elise.

"This isn't how this was supposed to go," Amber said against Raul's chest.

Elise pulled away from her mom. "You're right. I want to be ecstatic for you. I really do. But you blindsided all of us, Amber.

This is a life changing decision. For all of us. But even more so for me. We work together. All three of us. How does that relationship change?"

"It doesn't have to," Amber interrupted.

"Really? Our chef is going to be my brother-in-law. I've had all of one conversation with Raul that didn't revolve around food. And that was a conversation about the dining area set up. You don't think that relationship should change?" Elise asked.

Amber shrugged, the realization that she hadn't been fair to her sister finally dawning on her.

"And we live together. What does getting married mean for that?" Elise asked.

"We'll figure it out," Amber said.

Elise nodded. "I know we will. But this is a lot. I want to just be thrilled for you, but can't you see why this would take time for me to digest? Just like you hoped this whole scene would go differently, I've imagined the day you would tell me you were getting married as well. The guy would already be my best friend because how could I not love a guy who loved my favorite person in the world?"

Elise paused, not having to say she wasn't best friends with Raul.

"I get that this isn't about me. I'm trying to remember that," Elise said, tears coming down her cheeks again. "I really am happy that you're happy," she said as she sucked back a sob.

But she was so sad for herself. That much was easy to see. Nora hated this situation for all of them. She could see both sides so easily.

"I'm sorry, Elise," Amber said as she moved away from Raul.

But Elise shook her head. "Stay with your . . ." she paused, "Fiancé. I just need some time."

Elise stood. Amber ignored Elise's direction and walked a

few more steps, but Elise was quicker. She rushed from the room and went outside.

Amber looked back at the group that had watched mostly in silence.

"She just needs some time," Tabby reiterated.

Amber nodded but her eyes were red.

"She's right," Amber said.

"But you are too, sweetheart. This should have gone differently," Tabby said.

"It would have if I'd been sensitive to Elise. I just assumed this would be so fun. A big surprise. I didn't think through how it would affect Elise more than the rest of you. I should have told her I was dating Raul. I was just scared because I liked him so much. I didn't want to do anything to ruin it," Amber explained as she moved back to her fiancé's side.

Tabby nodded. "I get it. I think we all get it."

Nora joined the nods around the table.

"We're all pretty shocked, but she'll get used to the idea as we all will. In time," Tabby said. "I think we all just need some time."

Amber nodded before burying her head in Raul's chest once more. Nora loved the immediate comfort he gave her. She just wished Elise were receiving some sort of comfort as well. Both sisters seemed equally hurt, and both didn't deserve it.

But Tabby was right. In time, all would be well.

CHAPTER TWO

LOU LOOKED up at the clock, the one they'd received as a wedding present. Reminders of Lou's marriage dotted every part of her home. But it hadn't made sense to take down the clock just because Harvey had left her. A clock like the gorgeous one her aunt had given them would require hundreds of dollars to replace. And then there were the family pictures, but they had to stay up on the walls also. Harvey, the cheating scumbag, was still the father of her kids. Even if he hardly ever acted like one.

She figured she could at least take down the framed photo of the beautiful gazebo where she and Harvey had been married. But finding another sixteen-by-twenty-inch photo was such a pain.

A quick glance at the clock again brought her thoughts back to the present. She hadn't looked at the clock to remind herself of her failed marriage. She'd needed to see how much longer she had until it was time to pick up her kids from school. Forty-five minutes. Plenty of time to hide the evidence and take the five-minute drive to their school.

Now that all four were in elementary school, she had the morning to herself—an upside of having four kids in six years.

Although, if you'd told that to Lou of yesteryear when she'd been trying to juggle a five-, three-, two-year-old and newborn, she might've bitten her head off. Typically, Lou spent all those hours of freedom at her office in the gym where she worked, but today, she just couldn't go in. She didn't have it in her to smile at the gym's patrons who were all working out and living healthy lifestyles, while she hid a secret none of them could understand.

The secret, which lay all around her in the form of empty ice cream containers, empty candy bar wrappers, and empty bags of chips. Lou's binge today had been one for the record books. She'd never felt more ready to pop. Her throat constricted against the amount of food she'd consumed.

Lou shifted, the waistband on her sweatpants straining against the ever-widening girth of her waist. When had she become this woman? When Harvey left her, that was when.

She tried to swallow back the unadulterated fury she felt toward the man who had promised to adore her forever. He'd thought it so cute to change their wedding vows to add the word *adore*. He'd said no other word conveyed just what he felt for Lou. She'd eaten up all of the promises Harvey had freely given. Only to have him just as freely forget about them.

Lou shook the chip bag nearest her and found a few still at the bottom. Even as her body ached from the amount of food she'd consumed, she popped in those last few chips, promising herself that tomorrow she'd eat better. Maybe even work out. But after Harvey had broken every promise to her, why shouldn't she do the same to herself?

How many times had Harvey told Lou he'd take the kids and never shown up? How many times had Harvey said he'd fix something around the house only for Lou to have to call someone weeks later when said thing was still broken? How many times had Harvey cheated on her?

That was a question Lou didn't know the answer to. She'd

seen it with her own eyes once. But even after she'd caught Harvey red-handed on a date when he was supposed to be with his family, he still denied it. Said he loved her, cared for her. And then promptly ignored her for three months when she didn't respond to his two text messages filled with declarations of forever.

And because Harvey continued to lie, Lou never got her answers. The answers that would liberate her. Instead, she was consumed with doubts, wondering *what if?* What had she done to drive him into the arms of another? Why wasn't she enough? How many women? What had he done with those women? Did she know them? Get her groceries from them, talk to them at her gym, or wave to them at school pick-up?

She would never know.

Lou threw the book she'd attempted to start reading toward her fireplace. The paperback bounced off the stone and fell onto the beige carpet she'd been meaning to replace for months. Four kids meant having carpet that needed to be replaced frequently.

For two seconds, Lou felt badly about how she'd treated the book. Her mother—an avid reader and book lover when she'd been alive—would have been appalled. She used to get frustrated when Lou even dog-eared a book. But then again, the book Lou had thrown was a romance. She got enough of those kinds of lies from Harvey. She didn't need some author telling her she could have a happily ever after, as well. Those didn't exist for people like Lou.

But were there even others like her? Or was she the only person on this earth destined to be alone? Or worse, with a man who used her and then took off?

Lou's stomach twisted with scorn. She hated Harvey.

The doorbell rang, causing Lou to jump. Could it be that the kids had found a ride home?

Lou looked up at the clock. She still had half an hour. She was good. So who could it be?

Her best friend and step-sister, Alexis, was working. So were most of her other friends. The ones who didn't work would be too busy getting things wrapped up before picking up their kids to just drop by at this time. Her dad was now retired, but he and his wife, Margie, always called before coming over.

Lou would typically be glad for any visitor. But not today. Not when she still had evidence strewn all around her living room. Maybe it was a delivery person? Whoever it was, she'd just wait until they moved on.

Impatient knocking sounded, and she knew exactly who it was even though he hadn't been on her doorstep for months now.

"I know you're in there, Lou. You left the garage door open again, and I see your van," Harvey yelled through the door.

"Crap," Lou muttered, the closest thing to a swear word she ever said anymore. She'd had quite the potty mouth once upon a time, but with little ears always around, Lou had tamed her language over the years.

"I'm not going anywhere," Harvey continued yelling.

Why was he here? Today of all days? How many times had Lou called him, asking him to take their kids on his court appointed days? He'd never shown. He had texted once to say his life was really busy. He'd started dating the woman he claimed he hadn't been cheating with, Felicity. He hadn't even taken the time to tell Lou before the news hit town and she'd been given the hot gossip by Felicity's best friend, Jamie. Jamie had gloated like no other, and Lou had pretended that she couldn't care less. At least for all the island knew, he and Lou had been divorced for years at the time. No one other than Alexis knew that Lou had started dating the . . . words that Lou no longer said flitted through her mind . . . again. How Harvey could claim he hadn't cheated and then be dating the very woman Lou had seen him out with, Lou didn't know. But did Harvey explain anything to her? Of course not.

The knocking came again, this time even louder.

"I still have my key, Lou. I'll use it if you don't let me in. Or better yet, I can keep yelling everything I have to say. I'm sure the neighbors are loving the show."

Harvey's words had Lou hurrying to her front door. One, he could make good on his threat—Lou had never demanded he give back his key nor had she changed the locks since Harvey had moved out. And two, their neighbors would be straining to hear every word Harvey was yelling. Lou appreciated each one of the people who lived around her, but man were they all gossips.

"What do you want?" Lou hissed through the door, barely containing her dislike for the man on the other side.

He was lucky she wasn't able to open the door. If she did, Lou wasn't sure Harvey would be able to walk for a week.

"It's good to see you, too. Although I can't see you. Maybe you'll open the door?" Harvey asked, his voice easy and breezy.

She hated him.

"Remember what Alexis did to you?" Lou asked, suddenly feeling a little cheerier after being reminded of the day her best friend had elbowed Harvey in the nose. "I'll hit a place a whole lot more delicate if I open the door. Consider this door between us your friend."

Harvey laughed.

He had the audacity to laugh. When Lou meant every word of what she'd said.

"You've always been so cute when you're mad," Harvey said as if what was between them was merely a marital spat, not years of pain and hours of tears.

"What do you want, Harvey?" Lou spat. She needed to get

away from him. To not be able to see how unaffected he was by all that had happened between them, even though those same events had absolutely broken her.

"I want us again, Lou," Harvey said.

Lou froze. It felt as if a hand had literally taken her heart and squeezed it. She slid down the door and fell to the floor. Is this what she'd taught Harvey? That he could leave her for months, date someone else, ignore her and, worse, their children and then just come back?

"I know I messed up. I shouldn't have dated Felicity. But you wouldn't talk to me. You were accusing me of such awful things, and Felicity told me I was right. That I shouldn't be with a woman who didn't trust me. Funny, since she's the one who won't trust me now. Can you believe she accused me of cheating on her? Women," Harvey continued.

Did he know who he was speaking to? Did he know what each word was doing to Lou's soul? Did he know he was crushing her bit by bit? Any part of her she'd built up after he'd left was now gone. Crumbled to pieces under his careless words.

"I know the kids miss me, Lou. I know you miss me. I miss you too. Do you remember Sunday mornings?"

Memories of lying in bed and sharing sweet kisses until the kids came barging in filled Lou's mind.

Why was he doing this? He was twisting those beautiful memories. Using them in this most awful of moments. Now Lou would always associate those last blessed memories of their marriage with this. The time that Harvey thought Lou was worth so little that she'd come back to him now.

"I hate you," Lou finally found the strength to whisper.

"What?" Harvey asked.

He hadn't heard her. It had taken everything in her to say those words, and he hadn't heard her.

"I hate me," Lou again only whispered. But for some reason,

those words were easier to say. Did that mean they were more true?

"Lou, honey, I can't hear you. And now Mrs. Jenkins is getting her mail again. Just let me in. I promise I'll make this right."

Lou scoffed as her chest ached.

Make this right? How? She'd been trying for months to make any part of this even just bearable. She'd failed.

"Go away," Lou pleaded. She needed Harvey to leave.

"You don't mean that, Lou. We're good together, you and me. After all is said and done, no matter how many times we drift apart, we'll always be you and me."

There it was. Evidence that this time apart that had nearly made her give up on life was nothing to him. Merely a blip in their marriage. And worse, that it would happen again. Probably again and again. If Lou let Harvey back in, she would be here again all too soon.

She'd said she hated Harvey, but part of her wondered *what if?* What if she let him in? What if they tried again? What if their kids had their dad again? She hated that she was robbing them of him.

But she wasn't robbing them. He was. His decisions. Not Lou's. If he could be faithful and fulfil his promises to his children, Lou would take him back in an instant. But she knew he wouldn't. He would always be this man. The one who would try to love them for a few weeks and then lose interest. Because they would never be enough for him. And that wasn't Lou's fault.

The ache from her chest began to spread to her throat and stomach. Time was ticking, and she had to act now. She didn't think she could do it for herself, but she would do it for her kids.

"Leave, Harvey. The kids will be out of school soon. You can come back in an hour and finally spend time with them. They deserve more than you've been."

"You're the one who pushed me away, Lou. This isn't on me."

Lou felt fury build up within her.

"You left me and then you ignored our children. You cheated and then you left again, pretending as if all five of us never existed. That is *all* on you." Lou tried to rein in her anger and resentment to focus on what really mattered, the relationship Harvey had with their children. She drew in a deep breath before she spoke again. "But the cheating and leaving are our problems. They need to stay between us. Maybe we'll work on them one day. But for the time being, we'll put them aside to focus on our children. Because it's what parents do. It would be nice if you would finally man up, Harvey."

Lou knew the moment it was out that she shouldn't have said the last sentence. She was being petty, but she'd only been able to bite back so much frustration. So some of it had leaked out, and she'd insulted Harvey instead of keeping the conversation one-hundred percent constructive. Then again, she'd only spoken the truth. Maybe she'd said exactly what needed to be said.

Lou felt and heard a hand slam against the other side of the door, interrupting her thoughts. She guessed Mr. Nice Guy was gone.

"Don't you start calling me names. I deserve better than that." His words paused as his hand slammed against the door again. "I deserve better than you. But I chose you all those years ago, so I'm trying to do my best by you."

Lou felt each word slice her. Harvey had never been so brutally honest. Sure, he'd called her names, told her she was fat, pointed out that other women were more beautiful. But this was different. She'd always suspected he thought he deserved better than her, but to hear it from his mouth?

Yet those oozing wounds gave her more strength to focus on what was important. More and more, Lou was realizing that what had been between herself and Harvey wasn't worth saving. Other than the four incredible gifts her marriage had given her. So she would fight for them and forget herself and her own hurts.

"From now on, Harvey, this—any communication between us—is for our children. Call or text me when you want to see them. I'll have them ready. They miss you. You're right about that. Give them your best. Because they deserve that and so much more. But that will be the only communication between us. Because we. Are. Done."

Harvey had to understand that.

Another slam against the door told her he did.

"You'll regret this, Lou," Harvey yelled before pounding footsteps told her he was leaving.

Then he was gone. And Lou was left with pieces of herself.

But even as she ached to cry, she knew she had no time to do so. So she shoved away every hurt and emotion, stood up mechanically, and began to clean her living room, trying to erase Harvey's words that played over and over in her mind.

Because of all the words said, only a few mattered right then. Her kids deserved better. And Lou would do her very best to give them that.

CHAPTER THREE

JULIA SLID the sheet pan of potatoes into the oven, feeling immense pride. She was cooking. For many people this would be an average Thursday evening. But for Julia, each time she made something edible, it was an event to be celebrated. She'd honed a lot of skills over the years, but the kitchen had never been her domain—even though she'd played the part of a chef in a movie twenty years ago. She'd taken the role before she'd become adamant about method acting.

The potatoes that were now in her beautiful oven gleamed with the oil that Julia had slathered them in. She'd learned recently that fat was flavor and now maybe took it a little too far, if the scale could be believed. But even with the weight gain, according to her boyfriend, Ellis, she looked better than ever. And though she wasn't sure she completely believed him, his assurance that she was beautiful was always a confidence boost.

Maybe one day Julia would just know that she was a beautiful woman without needing assurance, but after years of being told she needed to do this or that in order to achieve the world's standards of visual perfection, it was hard to feel good about herself when she knew she'd always fall short. She was trying to learn, little by little, that that standard didn't matter. Man, who knew retirement would be a time so full of growing.

Julia's straying thoughts rounded back around to what she needed to focus on in that moment: dinner. Now that the potatoes were in, it was time to focus on her arch nemesis.

Chicken.

Julia loved poultry. It was often her greatest source of protein. But how did one cook the dang thing without serving it raw or overcooked. To Julia, chicken was as big of a mystery as the perfectly ripe avocado. Others were able to serve her these glorious culinary delights, but so far she'd been stumped.

But not today. Today she would prevail. At least in the chicken category.

She'd found a recipe on the internet: fool-proof oven-baked chicken. She'd read that the process was to coat the chicken in salt and pepper and then in a sauce before adding a pecan crust. Put that in an oven at three-hundred and fifty degrees until it reached the right internal temperature, and then let it rest. Apparently, rest was an important thing for meat.

Julia eyed the chicken. She could do this. She would do this. She'd promised Ellis a nice home-cooked meal this evening. He'd been in the studio all day with his writing team, coming up with songs for his new album. He'd claimed the process was going better than usual, thanks to his new muse. Julia wasn't sure she was worthy of that role, so she was trying to do more, be a better girlfriend. And that started with feeding her boyfriend who was passionate about food of all sorts.

Julia began to make the honey mustard sauce she would use to adhere the crust to the chicken when she reread the recipe. She had pretty much memorized the thing but didn't want to miss a single step.

"Shoot," Julia yelped as she saw that she had indeed missed something.

"I have to dry it," Julia muttered to herself as she grabbed a paper towel and began patting the chicken. She had no idea what this step would do, but it was important. At least to the woman sharing this recipe.

Just as Julia was elbow deep in raw chicken, her phone rang.

"Are you kidding me?" Julia said, eyeing her phone that was on a far counter of the kitchen. She'd put it there to keep it away from all the chicken juices. What was she supposed to do now?

Suddenly she remembered that Ellis had connected her phone to her virtual assistant, which was wired throughout her home. Apparently, all Julia had to do was say *answer my phone* and she could speak to whoever was on the other end. Mind blowing.

"Answer my phone," Julia said, and she was greeted with sobbing.

What in the heck?

Because Julia's phone had been so far away, she hadn't seen the caller ID. She had no idea who this was. By the tone of the crying, she was guessing it was a woman. But who would call her crying? Was this an emergency? Julia should've washed her hands, but now she felt stuck.

"Hello?" Julia greeted, at a loss as to what else she could do.

"Aunt Julia?" the voice on the other end asked.

"Wendy?" Fortunately, there was only one female who called her Aunt Julia, but it hadn't been a call she'd been expecting. She wasn't just surprised that her niece was calling her crying, she was surprised that her niece was calling her at all.

Julia had been estranged from her family for years and had only recently started developing relationships with some of them. She was now talking to her mother once a week and her brother or sister-in-law at least each month. But Julia still didn't have the best relationship with Wendy's mother, Lacey, even though anytime Julia visited her hometown of Travers, Wendy was on her list of people to see. Julia loved each of her nephews and niece, but they weren't really on calling terms. It seemed that now they were.

"What's going on, Sweetheart?" Julia asked, wondering if she needed to book a flight home.

Was it Julia's mom?

No. She'd just lost her dad a few months before. She couldn't lose someone else so quickly. Not when she'd just gotten her mom back.

"I'm sorry I'm crying. I thought I would be okay, but then I started thinking again about what happened. Ugh!"

Julia was grateful to hear the anger in Wendy's tone. That had to mean everyone was alive and well, didn't it?

"Is everything okay?" Julia asked, needing a clear answer before she could go on.

"It's my mom," Wendy replied.

Lacey? She wasn't sick, was she? Wendy's tone implied that it was frustration she felt toward her mother, not worry, but Julia needed to hear the words.

"Is she alright?" Julia ventured.

"She's fine. She's just trying to control my life. The way she always does," Wendy said.

Julia breathed a sigh of relief. She felt badly that Wendy was upset but was grateful everyone was well. Now she could focus on the call and maybe even finish cooking dinner while she did so. Ellis would be there any minute, and Julia really wanted this in the oven before he got there.

Julia was about to respond to Wendy when she continued.

"I'm stuck, you know?" Wendy asked.

Julia wasn't sure how to respond to that. She didn't know

how Wendy was stuck. Thankfully, Wendy didn't need Julia to say anything as she spoke yet again.

"I live in this tiny town. I have for my whole life. I even went to the TCC instead of leaving for college because it was what my mom wanted. I worked at the bank, and now I've been promised the position of manager by next year. It would be the top of the career ladder for me. I've dated what feels like every boy in town, and I'm only twenty-three. I've achieved absolutely everything I can here. At twenty-three. I mean, Mom wants me to get married and have three kids, but then what? And I don't even know if I want to get married. Mom keeps reminding me that I'm losing eggs every year that I'll never get back. I get that she got married when she was twenty-one. That she loves the life she leads. The same one that Grandma led and probably her mom before that."

Julia nodded even though Wendy couldn't see her. Wendy was right. It was the life Julia's Grandma had led as well. Except her grandma had had four kids.

While Wendy had spoken, Julia had quietly washed her hands, sauced her chicken and then crusted it. She examined it before deeming it done and sliding it into the oven, along with a tray of green beans. Now all she had to do was flip the chicken about halfway through its cooking time and it should be good. She was doing this. All while helping her niece. Granted, she hadn't done anything for Wendy yet, but she would. Yes! Julia kind of felt like superwoman.

"You understand, don't you, Aunt Julia?" Wendy asked.

Oh boy, did she. Except Julia had felt the way Wendy did when she was about sixteen. Living in that town for two more years had been near torture. She'd had to get out. And her family hadn't forgiven her for years. It was all water under the bridge now—well, except with Lacey—but it had been a hard road to travel. One Julia wasn't sure she wanted Wendy to traverse as well.

"I do," Julia said slowly. "I think the most important question you ask yourself now is 'What do you want, Wendy?' I heard a whole lot about what you don't want, but until you know what you do want, you can't really move forward."

"Yes! I'm so glad you get it. But that's my problem. I don't know what I want other than I want to see more. This town is such a tiny corner of the world. It's my mom's whole world. She wants it to be mine too, but . . ." Wendy paused, so Julia checked the time. She still had five minutes until she had to flip her chicken.

"When Grandpa died," Wendy continued, "I realized he'd lived a good full life. He was happy. He married the woman he loved, divorced the woman he loved, but then figured out how to be a friend to her. He had his kids and grandkids who loved him. He had a legacy in this town. He lived the life he wanted to live. Then I thought about me. What if I died right now? I knew I couldn't say the same thing. This isn't the life I want to live. But I don't feel like I'll know the life I want to live until I leave this place."

Julia could understand that. But it still made her nervous. Leaving her family behind was going to be a truly difficult step for Wendy. She couldn't know how hard until she did it, the way Julia had. But it had always been what had to be done for Julia because she *had* to go to Hollywood. She *had* to be an actress. There had been no plan B in her life. Thankfully, she'd achieved all she'd set out to do. But to leave Travers just to leave Travers? Did Wendy really want to do that?

"Your mom is going to be hurt. I know I don't have to tell you that she still doesn't speak to me," Julia said as she kept her eyes on the clock.

"I know," Wendy whispered. "I don't want to hurt her. But this isn't about her."

Wendy was right. And Julia had to support that. Even if it would further hurt her relationship with her sister. Wendy had to live her life for her. Or she'd be filled with regrets. Even though Julia's road had been far from perfect, she had no regrets because she'd lived the life she had wanted. And her niece deserved the same.

There was a light knock at the front door, and a few moments later, Julia looked up to see Ellis joining her in the kitchen.

"The phone," Julia mouthed, pointing to her virtual assistant and then grinning at her boyfriend.

Seeing him never got old. Ellis looked delicious in his gray Henley and what Julia called his cowboy jeans. His dark hair was rumpled from the many times he'd run his hand through it during the day. Ellis was ever pushing his hair out of his eyes, but Julia loved the longer length.

"Aunt Julia?" Wendy asked.

Right, her call. She was a terrible aunt.

"I'm here, Wendy," Julia said.

Ellis stood beside her, putting his arm around her and pressing a kiss to her temple.

"I knew you would be," Wendy said, sounding more upbeat than she had the rest of the conversation. "I want to be responsible in all of this. I'm not just fleeing life here without a plan. I already started looking up jobs on the island. Your bank needs a new teller. I felt it was serendipitous, but I needed you to approve first. I knew you would, though, because you get this. No one else does, but I knew you would. I know Whisling is still small, but it's a new place, new people, and new scenery. I've longed to live near a beach my whole life. I'll be seeing a different way of life, right?"

"Right," Julia managed. What the heck was happening?

"Then if I live on Whisling and decide Travers is where I really want to end up, I'll know it wasn't because it was the only option. I would know Travers is for me, you know?"

"Yeah," Julia said as Ellis chuckled. She was glad he saw humor in all of this. Had Wendy said she was going to live on Whisling?

"I won't be staying with you forever. But I knew you'd be a soft place to land. I don't know that I'd be brave enough to do this all alone. I'm so glad I have you, Aunt Julia," Wendy said too quickly. Julia couldn't get a word in edgewise. Not that she had anything to say. She was still a little stunned by the turn of conversation.

"I'll book my flight tonight and let you know the details. Oh man, mom will be livid. But I have to do this. Thank you for taking my side," Wendy said so sincerely that Julia couldn't reply that she didn't want to take sides in this. She figured she kind of already had since she hadn't talked Wendy out of moving to Whisling. Honestly, the idea of having family close wasn't a bad one. Julia was warming to it more by the second.

"I fly into Seattle and then take a ferry to Whisling, right?" Wendy asked.

"Yeah," Julia said.

"That is so cool!" Wendy said.

Julia remembered her own overjoyed feeling when she'd heard the mode of transport to the island. It really was cool.

"Is it okay to be scared?" Wendy asked, her exuberance dropping by about a hundred percent.

"It is," Julia said, the memory of the day she'd left Travers forever seared in her mind. "I was nearly out of my mind with fear. But I realized the only thing that scared me more than leaving Travers was staying."

"That's exactly how I feel," Wendy said quietly, seeming consumed by her thoughts.

"You sure you want to do this?" Julia had to ask.

"I have to do this," Wendy replied.

It was the answer Julia needed to hear.

"Then I'll be making up my guest bedroom for you tonight. My door is always open to you," she promised.

"I love you, Aunt Julia. I'll be in contact soon."

"I love you," Julia replied before Wendy ended the call.

"Well," Ellis said after a few moments of silence. Julia was still cuddled at his side.

"Looks like I'll be having a houseguest," Julia said brightly. She really was thrilled about Wendy coming.

"But?" Ellis asked. He knew there was more. She loved that this man knew her so well.

"I'm worried for her. Lacey won't take this well. Her kids are her whole world. And she lashes out when she feels any difficult emotion. I don't want to see Wendy get hurt."

Ellis kissed the top of Julia's head. "That's what makes you such a great aunt and the woman I am madly in love with."

Julia grinned. She should've known Ellis would make everything feel like it was going to be okay.

"She'll be fine. And thankfully, she has it much better than you did. She has an aunt in the big, bad world ready to be by her side."

That was true. Wendy would never feel as alone as Julia had. Julia could promise her that.

"Thank you," Julia said, gazing up at her man.

"Thank you. Because based on that smell, dinner is going to be delicious," Ellis replied.

"The chicken!" Julia yelped as she ran out of Ellis's arms and toward the oven.

Julia sighed as she opened the oven. It was too late to flip the chicken. Fortunately, the crust hadn't burned. But the chicken wasn't moist or juicy, the words the recipe had said the dish would be if Julia cooked it just right. It looked like tonight wouldn't be the night Julia perfected chicken.

However, she'd been able to support her niece. That had been so much more important. If she had to make the choice again, she'd make the same one every time.

But Julia wasn't giving up. She would win the battle against chicken. It would just have to be some other night.

CHAPTER FOUR

THE FRONT DOOR SLAMMED SHUT, and Piper looked up from her spot on the couch to see Kristie walk into the living room. Kristie was finally home. It felt like Piper had been waiting for this moment for months.

Joy filled her as she jumped up and gave her daughter the kind of hug that only family who had been parted for far too long could give. Piper wasn't sure why she felt the need to hug her daughter for such a long time, but Kristie didn't begrudge her.

"Were you out with Brock?" Piper asked about Kristie's boyfriend, still hugging her because she was unwilling to let go. Was that why she hadn't seen Kristie much? Kristie and her boyfriend had been getting really close, but for some reason, Piper wasn't worried about it being too much too soon.

"No. I have some new friends now," Kristie said.

Piper couldn't see her face, but she could feel her daughter's smile. She turned her head so that she could take in every aspect of her daughter's face. Kristie seemed more grown up than the last time Piper had seen her and totally at peace.

"That's great," Piper said, returning Kristie's smile.

"It is," Kristie said.

"I missed you," Piper said, unsure where the words had come from. But she had. So much.

"I know." Tears glistened in Kristie's eyes. "I missed you too, Mom."

Piper let out a sob, suddenly overcome with emotion. Had it been the tears in Kristie's eyes that had prompted it? Maybe. But it was more than just that. Deep down Piper knew it was.

And even as Piper couldn't help but cry, she also wanted to push it away. She knew this wasn't something she wanted to waste her time doing. Not now.

"But things are really great where I'm at. I'm happy," Kristie said, squeezing her mother tightly as she spoke, the gesture somehow both reassuring and heartbreaking.

Piper nodded. She could feel that too. "And at peace," she said, stating her earlier observation.

"I am," Kristie said with a nod.

Why did it appear that Kristie had aged at least a year since Piper had last seen her? She couldn't have been gone for that long, could she?

"You look beautiful," Piper told her little girl who wasn't such a little girl anymore.

"You do too, Mom. But you also look worn out. And sad," Kristie said softly.

Piper knew that was the truth. She'd been sad for a long time. Until Kristie had come back just moments before, Piper hadn't been feeling at peace. Something had gone terribly wrong. Something Piper would never be able to fix.

"I know. But I don't know how to be happy anymore." Piper revealed a truth she hadn't known she was hiding. "I feel like the best part of me is gone."

But that didn't make sense. Kristie was right here. And she'd always been the best part of Piper.

"One part, Mom. Not the best part. The best part of you is the part of you that loves me. And she'll never be gone."

Piper felt tears stream down her cheeks. Kristie's words pierced her soul.

"If you were ever to leave me, that part would be gone," Piper argued.

Kristie smiled as she wiped away her mom's tears. "I know you're almost always right, Mom. But this time I know I am. That part of you can never leave, even when I'm gone."

When? Why was Kristie saying *when?* She couldn't leave. Piper wouldn't survive that. But Piper couldn't dwell on that as Kristie spoke again.

"That beautiful part is in each and every one of our memories. Even the one when you lied to me to get me to the dentist, and I cried for weeks that I couldn't trust you anymore." Kristie grinned, so Piper did too. "That part continues to grow, Mom. Even now. Each time you smile at a kid who is sad and brighten their day. Each time you decide your pain is less important than the pain of someone around you. Each time you look at dad."

"It doesn't feel like that," Piper said, her mind at odds with what she could see. Kristie had been gone. And even though she was back now, Piper suddenly realized she'd be gone again soon.

She held her daughter close once more, trying to keep from ever having to let go.

"I need you to find happiness again, Mom," Kristie said into Piper's shoulder.

"I can't." The tears running down Piper's cheeks wouldn't stop.

"You can. Stop feeling guilty every time you begin to move on. I want that for you. It's what I'm doing."

"How do I move on?" Piper asked the question she'd never been able to answer.

"Keep doing what you're doing, but try to find joy while you do it. You love photography. Don't forget that. Eat a cheese-burger, milk shake, and fries and savor every bite. Let Dad in."

This was the second time Kristie had mentioned Carter.

"He left us, Kris," Piper said.

"But he's back. And he's not going anywhere this time. You know that."

Piper did. But it hadn't seemed right to find happiness with Carter when Kristie wasn't around to enjoy it.

"He needs you. And you need him. Life will never be the same. But it can be just as incredible. If you'll let it."

Piper shook her head. There was no way. Kristie was gone. She wasn't sure where or why Kristie had gone, but she could feel it was the truth. Her daughter had left her. And life would never be as full without Kristie there.

"I'm always with you. Here." Kristie pointed at Piper's heart. "We won't ever let each other go."

"But if I'm happy again, that's exactly what I've done."

Kristie laughed. "Mom, of all the silly things. When you hold my hand, when you hold me in your arms and then do something that makes you happy, are you letting me go?"

It wasn't the same thing.

"You can hold on to me and find your happiness. I need you to do that, Mom."

Why wouldn't these tears stop?

"Promise me you'll do that, Mom."

Piper would do anything for her daughter. Even this. She guessed with how important this was to Kristie, she especially had to do this.

But Piper didn't want to give in yet. She somehow knew the moment she did, Kristie would be gone.

"Kristie—"

"We don't have much more time. Please, Mom."

Kristie was going to leave her again. She had to leave. How

could Piper let this happen? Yet she knew in her heart she could do nothing to stop it. She hated the helpless feeling that overwhelmed her. But she'd give her daughter what she wanted. She would do this. For Kristie.

"I promise," Piper whispered.

Kristie grinned.

"I love you, Mom. Everything will be okay. On some days great. On others, not so good. And then we'll be together again."

"Promise?" Piper asked.

"I promise," Kristie returned. "Be happy. Laugh a lot, cry a little. That's how it's supposed to be. That's what I'm doing."

Suddenly Kristie was gone from her arms, walking to the door again.

"No!" Piper said, reaching toward her daughter.

"Just for a time, Mom. I'll see you again."

Piper dropped her arms, feeling the truth of Kristie's words. Kristie was just leaving for a time. Piper would see her again. Kristie somehow knew it, so now Piper did too.

Piper felt her bed sheets around her. Was she lying down? How had that happened?

Her eyes opened, taking in the darkness of the room. It had all been a dream.

But it had felt so real. Piper could practically feel the way Kristie had felt as she'd hugged her, the smell of her strawberry shampoo. Was that all just from Piper's memories?

"Be happy," Piper heard whispered near her ear.

And then she knew the truth. It hadn't been a normal dream. She'd seen Kristie. She knew it in her soul. She wouldn't tell others because they would doubt. But Piper would always know the truth. Kristie had come to her. Comforted her and extracted a promise Piper wasn't sure she knew how to keep.

But she would keep it.

CHAPTER FIVE

TEN GONGS CHIMED from Alexis's grandfather clock. The new acquisition had been expensive. And now Alexis completely regretted it.

She had searched through every antique store from here to Seattle. At the time, she hadn't been sure why she was so adamant that she have this exact type of clock in her home. The antique didn't fit her aesthetic, but she'd gotten the idea into her head and hadn't stopped searching until she'd found this precise one. One that not only chimed on the hour, but each and every second, the ticking could be heard—even on the other side of the living room.

Now that she had the clock in her home, she knew exactly why she'd bought the monstrosity. She'd wanted noise other than her own at home with her. Ever since her mom had moved out, things had become quiet. And then even quieter when she and Jared had decided now was not the right time for them to date. Without a mom or boyfriend around, Alexis had resorted to having the TV on all the time—anything to make her home seem a little less hollow. When that grew old, she decided to acquire this huge grandfather clock, which she'd had to hire special delivery drivers to bring all the way to the island.

But the clock had been a bad move. Now she jumped every hour, and although she would probably get used to it, the constant ticking of the seconds weren't the comfort she'd hoped more noise would bring. Instead, she was reminded of how quickly or slowly the seconds of life were ticking by.

Honestly, what she should have done was bought a dog. Alexis's heart warmed imagining a cute little pup next to her, but that could never be. She worked too many hours at the food truck she loved to be what a dog needed. She'd just gotten home from a fourteen-hour day because her boss, Bess, had had to leave early. That happened quite often, and although Alexis never minded the long hours of work—in fact, she loved them—leaving a dog alone for hours on end wasn't fair. Alexis shouldn't have a dog for the very reason she wanted one. Her house was just too empty.

She picked up her phone, knowing what she was going to do next even while avoiding it. She'd put all her memories of her time with Jared in a box that was in the crawl space above her house. The place creeped her out, so Alexis knew banishing them up there meant she wouldn't be reliving memories when she needed to move on. But the one thing she'd allowed herself to keep near her were the photos on her phone. She couldn't bring herself to erase them or even put them on a hard drive that she couldn't access easily. She needed the comfort of having even just that tiny part of Jared near her.

So she clicked on her photo album and smiled the moment Jared's handsome face filled her screen. He'd been hers. Sometimes it was hard for Alexis to believe that. He was attractive, for sure, but Jared was so much more than that. He texted every acquaintance, including all his patients, on their birthdays—he had a calendar full of reminders so that he would never forget a person on their special day. He often dropped flowers off while Alexis was at work so that when she came home, yellow daffodils or purple roses would greet her. He still did that even though they'd broken up. And he was so funny. Alexis chuckled as she moved on to the next picture. Jared was mid-shake, Alexis having caught a moment while he was dancing. The man was good at many things, but dancing was not one of them. Yet he knew how much Alexis laughed when he attempted to bust a move, so he'd done so just for her.

She clutched her phone to her chest. She missed him. So much.

She'd seen him earlier that day. He'd gone to the food truck to pick up his lunch. But having him so close was almost harder. She ached with longing every time she saw him, but nothing could change. At least for a number of years. Because his children hated her. Or the idea of her. Either way, they'd been miserable when Jared and Alexis had dated, and it had caused such tension in their home that Alexis couldn't bear it. She couldn't be the reason Jared's relationship with his children suffered. They'd tried and tried again to win the kids over, but as long as Marsha, Jared's ex, was against it, poisoning their children against Alexis, nothing would change.

To have a man like Jared love her and then have to let him go? It had been and still was the worst thing she'd ever gone through. But she found goodness in every new day because it was what Jared had taught her.

Her phone vibrated against her chest, Lou's picture filling her screen.

Alexis sighed. She should've known Lou would call right now. The woman had a sixth sense, somehow knowing when Alexis was doing what she shouldn't, like reminiscing on times with Jared. Alexis knew if she answered, Lou would get it out of her that she'd been scrolling through old pictures and she'd be in for a scolding.

But even knowing that, Alexis had to answer. It was her best friend.

"Hello?" Alexis said as pandemonium hit her ear.

There was crying, yelling, and quite possibly a few cuss words coming from the other end of the call. What was going on?

"Lou. Where are you?" Alexis asked, instead of seeing if everything was alright. Obviously it wasn't.

"She's going to die!" Alexis heard a tiny voice say.

"Cash?" Alexis asked, assuming the voice was Lou's younger son. Who was going to die? Was Lou in trouble? Had Cash called Alexis?

"She's not dying," Alexis finally heard Lou say.

Alexis held a hand to her heart. Oh thank heavens. Lou was speaking and apparently no one was dying. But her heart was still beating rapidly from the scare. And Lou's voice had been strange, a tone Alexis had never heard. Something was still terribly wrong.

"Can you hear me, Lou?" Alexis asked, needing more answers.

Lou sniffled, and it took everything in Alexis not to join her crying friend. When Lou hurt, Alexis hurt, even if she didn't know why they were hurting.

"It's Marsha, Lexus," Lou said.

Alexis froze. Marsha? Were the kids okay? Jared? It was telling that the first image that came to Alexis's mind were the faces of Brittany and Peter, revealing to her that she hadn't fallen in love with just Jared.

"She was in a car accident," Aiden, one of Lou's sons, yelled.

Cries erupted. Alexis wasn't sure if those came from just the children or Lou as well.

"We're on our way to the hospital. Dad and Margie are too. Jared and his kids should already be there. We need you, Lexus," Lou said before a sob escaped.

Even as Alexis felt immense relief that everyone else was physically okay, especially Peter and Brittany, this was bad. Lou wasn't a dramatic person. For her to be crying like this? Maybe Marsha was still alive but the outlook couldn't be good. This wasn't a fender bender.

"Hey, Emma," Alexis said since she was pretty sure she was on the car's sound system.

"Yes?" Lou's oldest asked tentatively, but her voice was steady. Just as Alexis imagined it would be.

"I need you to be strong for your Mama, okay? I'll be at the hospital as soon as I can, but until then, can I count on you?" Alexis asked, hating that she needed to ask this of an eleven-year-old. But Lou wasn't okay.

"Yes," Emma said with a sureness only a sweet eleven-year-old could.

"Awesome. And guys, guess what hospitals have. Vending machines," Alexis said as she searched her entryway for shoes, purse, and keys.

"Vending machines?" Hazel asked.

"The things that give candy," Aiden said, his voice a strange mixture of excitement and the ghost of tears.

"Everyone gets one trip to the vending machine with Aunt Alexis, okay?"

Cheers took place of the previous cries. Just as Alexis had suspected, the kids were responding more to their mother's fear than their own. The last thing Lou needed was to be worrying about her kids' hurts.

"Can I have M&M's?" Hazel asked.

"You can have whatever you want. Think about it until I get there, okay?"

"Okay," came a chorus of replies.

"Thank you, Lexus," Lou said before ending the call.

Crisis mode had helped Alexis not to think about what had actually happened. But as she drove, her thoughts strayed to why she was going to the hospital. Marsha, a woman with whom she had a very complicated relationship, was there. Recovering from a car accident. What had happened? When had it happened? How were Marsha's kids emotionally? Jared? Bill?

Alexis had known Marsha was tied to her, but it was in this very moment that it became clear just how intertwined their lives were. Marsha was the daughter of the man Alexis's mother loved. She was the sister of Alexis's best friend and, even more, she was now Alexis's step-sister. She was also the mother to Jared's children and the ex-wife of the man Alexis loved. Basically, every person who Alexis loved loved Marsha as well. And yet the woman hated her. And because of that, Alexis had allowed her own feelings toward the woman to sour. Not that she would ever wish this on Marsha.

Alexis groaned as she leaned her head back at a red light. Marsha would hate that Alexis was at the hospital. Would they be able to keep that a secret? Alexis doubted it. And yet she had to go. It hadn't even occurred to her to tell Lou she wouldn't show up. Lou needed her. Alexis was sure her mother would also need her. So Alexis would do her best to stay out of the way, avoid Jared, and care for those who needed her.

She felt a little like she was stuck in a web that she needed to carefully maneuver her way through. But one didn't maneuver in a web. One got stuck. Alexis sure hoped she wouldn't be getting stuck that night.

She pulled into the hospital and immediately found parking. She guessed that was the plus side of coming to the hospital at nearly eleven pm.

Wait, had Lou awakened her kids when she'd gotten the

news about Marsha? She should've called Alexis to babysit. Granted, they were barely into the new school year, and she knew for a fact Lou's kids had been on an awful schedule during the summer. Maybe they'd still been up?

Alexis had no idea why she was dwelling on such a ridiculous query when there were so many more important things to concern her. But it was almost like her mind needed to focus on the things that didn't matter or she would lose it too. And the last thing Alexis could do was lose it.

We're in the waiting room on the third floor. Lou's text came in just as Alexis walked into the hospital. She took the elevator up two floors, and as soon as the doors opened, she wished they would close once again. She hated the scene in front of her.

Her eyes went straight to Jared. She didn't want them to, but she couldn't help it. She had to see that he was okay.

Their gazes met from across the room. A flicker of a smile appeared on his lips. Alexis felt a pull toward the man like nothing she'd ever experienced before.

But something drew Jared's attention down, and thankfully, the spell that had been over her was broken. She would no longer do anything silly like jump into his arms.

Besides, they were a little full at the moment. Alexis realized that Jared's attention had been taken by Peter, whose face was against his dad's chest, Jared's arms encircling him.

Alexis's gaze moved to other parts of the scene. Brittany and Emma were embracing as they shared the chair next to Jared, Brittany's eyes raw from tears. Lou had her littles under each of her arms, and Aiden sat next to Peter, his eyes filled with concern for his elder cousin. Bill paced the floor, and Margie sat nearby, wringing her hands.

It was all so pitiful, and yet Alexis knew she could do nothing to help. Not really.

"You came," Lou said as she looked up, her eyes nearly as red as Brittany's.

"Of course I came. I have all of these dollar bills just burning a hole in my wallet, and I heard the best vending machine in town is here," Alexis said, trying to sound upbeat yet somber at the same time. She knew it would hurt Brittany and Peter if she didn't sound sorrowful over the situation their mother was in. And even if she didn't have as much right as the others in that room, Alexis did feel true sorrow about what had happened to Marsha.

But Alexis had no need to worry. Neither of Jared's kids seemed to even notice that she'd entered the room, much less listened to her. They were in their own worlds of heartache.

Aiden perked up at Alexis's words, but the other three of Lou's kids didn't seem to hear her either. Alexis realized that seeing their cousins and grandpa in this state had to have affected them.

Even Aiden wasn't quite as eager as he had been in the car, but he did stand and walk slowly toward the seat Alexis now sat in, right next to Hazel.

"Do you guys want some candy?" Lou asked Hazel and Cash.

Hazel nodded, standing to join her brother. Cash didn't move.

"I think these vending machines have chips as well," Alexis said, remembering that Cash wasn't the biggest fan of sweets.

Cash didn't say anything but also stood, his movements slow.

Alexis handed each kid a few dollars. She wanted to give them much more, but she knew Lou wouldn't appreciate it.

"Thank you," all three said soberly before walking from the waiting room to the hall where they could see vending machines.

Alexis glanced over at Emma, who was still hugging her cousin. Alexis would give Emma her cash later.

With Hazel gone, Alexis moved one chair over and pulled Lou into a hug. Her friend sank into the embrace.

Lou didn't cry—Alexis was guessing she was trying to be strong in front of Peter and Brittany—but she allowed herself to be held.

They sat silently while Alexis waited for Lou to tell her anything more that she needed. Nothing came.

A sob sounded from the seats across from them, and Alexis looked up to see Peter stifling his cries with his father's chest. Jared's face wore a look of complete anguish as he tried to comfort his child.

Brittany had moved so that she was no longer hugging Emma but was instead snuggling against her Dad. Jared seemed at a loss as to how to care for either of his kids. Both were distraught.

Lou left Alexis's hug with a quickly said *thanks* before standing and taking the seat on the other side of Peter. Lou pulled Peter in at her side, allowing the young teenager a place of safety so that Jared could turn his attention to Brittany.

Alexis had never encountered such a scene in her life. And she hoped to never do so again.

Bill stopped his pacing and moved to take the seat on the other side of Emma and Brittany. As soon as Bill sat, Emma crawled out of the chair she'd been sharing with her cousin and onto her grandpa's lap.

Alexis realized they were just where they needed to be, so it was time for her to check on the younger kids.

She stood and started for the hall of vending machines when she was met by her mother.

"Hey, Mom," Alexis said softly, not wanting to disturb the quiet room.

Margie tugged her daughter into a hug and held her for a moment.

"How are you holding up?" Alexis asked. She and Margie were far enough away from the others to have a whispered conversation no one else would hear.

"Better than them." Margie looked toward the sorrowful group. Alexis did the same, and her eyes once again met Jared's. He stared at her so intently that Alexis physically felt it. He was telling her something she didn't quite understand. She had a feeling she'd hear it later though. Whatever it was was important.

"What happened?" Alexis asked, realizing she knew nothing other than that Marsha had been in a car accident.

"Marsha was driving twenty above the speed limit on Beach Road," Margie began.

Alexis knew that road well. People often sped on it because there was almost never any traffic. But the twists and turns held many blind spots, so it wasn't the smartest place to go so fast.

"She came around a turn and ran into the back of a car that was in the middle of the road due to a collision it had already been in. Thankfully, the drivers were already out of their cars and far enough away from the accident that they weren't hurt. And the whole thing wouldn't have been too bad if a huge truck didn't come around the corner right after Marsha, smashing her between the two vehicles."

"No," Alexis gasped. The tiny car Marsha drove would be no match for a truck. And to be sandwiched like that.

Margie nodded.

"Is the driver of the truck okay?" Alexis asked.

"Walked away with just a few cuts from when his windshield broke on him."

"And what do we know about Marsha?"

Margie shrugged. "An ambulance had to bring her here. Her

car was totaled. I guess the good news was that they didn't have to fly her to Seattle."

That *was* good news. Granted, Whisling's hospital was pretty amazing. It was only the direst of circumstances that made anyone need to leave the island for medical situations.

"Aunt Alexis, Aiden says I can only have candy or chips. Not both." Hazel's complaints came down the hall from the vending machines to where Alexis and Margie stood.

"Mom wouldn't want us to eat so much junk food this late at night," Aiden replied, following his sister.

"Typically, you'd be right, Aiden. But I think your mom would be okay with it tonight. Here, let me help you guys," Alexis said as she put an arm around either child and walked down the hall to where Cash was still staring at the vending machine, as if it were a puzzle to be solved.

Alexis looked down at the heads of the kids with her, the two blondes and one brunette. She loved them more than she could've imagined when she'd first met them a couple of years ago. But a lot had happened during those years.

Now that Alexis had given the kids permission to get whatever they wanted, it was a free for all. Cash punched in the code for two bags of chips, a pretzel mix, and a beef jerky stick. Hazel got her chips and M&M's, and Aiden did the opposite of his brother, choosing two bags of fruity candy and two more of chocolates.

Loaded with their treasures, the kids walked back toward the group who still sat waiting.

"You might want to share some of that," Alexis said as she appraised the loot. But she hadn't been able to tell the kids *no*, even when she'd run out of dollar bills and had to use a credit card to pay for Aiden's purchases.

"That's a good idea," Lou said as she plucked a bag of chocolates out of Aiden's hands. She'd moved from sitting next to

Peter back to her previous seat. Emma sat next to her, and Bill was with Margie next to them. Jared still sat in his same seat, hugging Peter and Brittany on each side of him.

Peter and Brittany had been so consumed by their grief that neither had seemed to notice Alexis's entrance earlier, but she saw on their faces that they could see her now. She waited for one to make a comment about her being there or to ask her to leave. She would do whatever they asked, even if Lou wanted her there. The kids' needs would have to take precedence. But each just watched her a moment before moving on to something else in the room. No looks of shock or horror, just acceptance. As if they'd expected her to be there.

Alexis didn't allow hope to bloom in her chest. Not tonight. It wasn't fair to any of them. But she knew she'd reflect on this moment a whole lot later.

She noticed Peter eye Cash's chips.

"Are either of you hungry?" Alexis asked Jared's kids.

Brittany shook her head and Peter noticed, slowly following suit.

"Well, if that changes, just let me know, okay?" Alexis said, trying to keep her voice as quietly kind as possible.

The kids nodded, neither smiling but neither crying either, so Alexis would count that as a win.

The sounds of bags opening filled the air as Lou's kids ripped into their spoils. She noticed Emma had swiped a bag of Cash's treats.

Lou handed the half-eaten bag of chocolate back to Aiden as she looked from her dad and Margie to Jared and then Alexis.

"Do any of you want a cup of coffee? I know hospitals are notorious for not having the best brews, but I feel like we could all use anything right about now," Lou said, seeming way less emotional than she had been before. Alexis was going to guess the grief would hit in waves. Right now, they were in the calm, but Alexis had a feeling another set of waves of sorrow would be hitting soon.

Bill nodded but paused as his eyes flew to the other side of the waiting room.

"Are you folks the family of Marsha Tuttle?" the doctor who'd just entered the room asked, and Bill jumped out of his seat. Margie and Lou did the same, all of them rushing to where the doctor stood.

Alexis glanced over to see Jared watching the group of adults. Even though he was no longer married to Marsha, he should be there. Especially as a doctor. He'd be able to understand things in a way none of the rest of them could.

Alexis met Jared's eyes and then motioned for him to join the others. Jared gave a barely perceptible shake of his head as he glanced at each of his kids.

Oh. Now she knew why he hadn't moved. But shouldn't he be in that huddle *because* of his kids? Yet, how could he leave them alone? All the other adults were gone.

Except for Alexis.

Knowing she could be in for a world of hurt but putting her fears behind her, Alexis stood and moved to where Jared sat.

"I think your dad should go talk with the doctor. Do you two mind if I take his place?" Alexis asked, her voice sounding too breathy. Too full of fear. But this was about the kids and Jared and Marsha.

Peter looked up first, confusion filling his eyes. Brittany then looked to Alexis as well, and it was easy to see she knew exactly what Alexis was asking.

Brittany's eyes bounced from her dad to the group by the doctor. She stared for a moment that felt like an eternity. Alexis was already shifting her weight so that she could walk back to her seat.

But Brittany nodded.

Peter had watched his sister and understanding dawned on him as well. He joined his sister in nodding.

Wait, had both kids just said Alexis could take the seat their father was in to try to comfort them?

Alexis would not celebrate. Even though this felt monumental.

A surprised but pleased looking Jared stood. "Thank you for coming," he whispered into Alexis's ear before moving a few steps so that she could take his black vinyl seat.

That had been the important message he'd been trying to convey earlier. Alexis was grateful she hadn't understood. She liked this form of delivery much better.

Focus on the kids and not the flutters their father gives you.

Alexis quickly turned her attention back to Peter and Brittany as she drew in a deep breath. She glanced from one teen to the other, but neither said a thing, so Alexis sat.

Jared nodded, shooting Alexis a slight smile before walking toward the doctor.

Alexis was pretty sure she'd never been so stiff in her life. But she didn't know what to do. Was she supposed to try to keep from touching either child?

Suddenly, Brittany leaned on her arm. Alexis lifted it to put it around her, Brittany snuggling further in at her side. Peter rested his head on Alexis's shoulder, and her heart nearly screamed with delight.

But then she remembered why the kids were so worn out and couldn't be ecstatic, although her pleasure wouldn't quite go all the way away.

Alexis wasn't sure what this meant. Or if this even meant anything. But for now, she would accept the moment for what it was. She had been able to give two children she loved comfort in their time of need.

CHAPTER SIX

"SHE'S MOVING," Amber said as soon as Nora let her daughter into her condo. When Nora had heard knocking, she'd assumed it was Mack on his way to work that morning. He often stopped by for just a few minutes before his shift, and even though it would have been nice to get a morning kiss from her boyfriend, Nora was pleasantly surprised to see Amber instead. Until she took in the stricken look on her daughter's face.

"Who's moving?" Nora asked, focusing back on Amber. The girl's normally perfectly coiffed hair was in a messy bun, and she wore a t-shirt and sweats. This wasn't her daughter's normal look for ten am.

"Elise. To Seattle. You know how we needed someone there? She decided she could be that someone. Without even talking to me about it," Amber said, throwing up her arms and then dropping them.

Nora opened her mouth to speak but Amber continued. "Does it matter to her that we have one of the biggest weddings of the decade coming up in less than six months?"

The girls had found out a little over a month before that the Hollywood starlet, Genevieve Porter, wanted to have her wedding on the island at their lodge. They had both been thrilled, even when Genevieve had said she wanted to have a January wedding, giving them not nearly enough time to plan. But the opportunity had been too incredible to pass up, even with all the extra hours they'd have to work. They were already toiling day in and day out to make sure all would go well for that.

"She said Raul and I would have that covered. That we need to look toward the future. 'What about after the wedding?' she asked. She said we need to make sure marketing plans are in place and our relationships in Seattle are kept up, despite our busy schedule," Amber spouted, throwing herself onto Nora's couch.

"She does have a point," Nora said, not sure what her daughter was looking for.

"I know she does!" Amber yelled. "That's not what I mean."

Okay. Then Nora was missing something. Maybe lots of somethings.

"She's moving," Amber said, sinking back.

Oh. That was what she was missing.

"We have an incredible staff, so I know work will be fine. But I won't be," Amber said, turning to her mom who had taken the seat beside her. "This is supposed to be about us."

"This?" Nora asked, sure she was lost again.

"The wedding."

Nora cringed because she knew she would have to say something Amber didn't like. "The wedding is about you and Raul."

"I know that," Amber said with an eye roll before curling up in a ball. "But the wedding planning. I'm not supposed to do that with Raul. Elise and I have had this pre-arranged for years. We would stay up late into the night, pouring over wedding magazines, watching romcoms. Doesn't she realize that after I get married nothing will be the same?"

"I'm sure she does. I can't be in Elise's head, but I imagine that might be *why* she's moving. Maybe she didn't realize how hard saying goodbye to this stage of life would be. You and Elise have been joined at the hip for most of your lives. You've always lived together, other than your college years. Now it will never be like that again. I'm sure she understands it's a joyful time, but she's also mourning what she's losing," Nora said, trying to be fair to both her girls.

"But why do it prematurely? It makes no sense. Unless she disapproves of this wedding or Raul. This is her way of saying she's totally against us, isn't it?"

Nora had no idea. But she had to say something. "What has she said?"

Amber shrugged. It was easy to see she was deep in her thoughts. "That she wants to be happy for me and she will be. But it all happened too fast."

Nora had to agree with that last sentence.

"Why is it happening so fast?" Nora asked. Amber had told her she was looking at a November wedding. That meant Amber and Raul would have met, started secretly dating, gotten engaged, and then married all in less than a year's time.

"I don't want it to be too close to Genevieve's wedding," Amber said quietly.

Nora eyed her daughter. She may have missed years of her life, but she could read her pretty well. Amber was hiding something.

"Then it could be in April." Nora stated the obvious.

"But when you know, you know. Why put it off?" Amber asked.

Nora understood that. She really did. But you didn't have to get married as soon as you knew. She told her daughter as much.

"I know," Amber said, her voice going quiet again.

"Do you want me to be honest with you?" Nora asked.

Amber narrowed her eyes at her mom, scrutinizing her. She finally nodded.

"I can tell you're hiding something. And it doesn't feel good. Especially about something as important as the man you are going to be with for the rest of your life. It makes me nervous and worried for you. Did Elise ask you if you're hiding something?" Nora asked.

Amber nodded.

"And you didn't tell her?"

"I told her I wasn't hiding anything. That I'm just in love," Amber said before biting her lip. "She knew I was lying. The next day she told me her decision to move to Seattle."

"I think she's hurt Amber. You kept dating Raul from her and now something else. She feels like these things are coming between the two of you, and she is trying to make that pain go away."

"By getting away from me," Amber muttered.

Nora nodded.

"But I can't tell her. She'll judge me and think it's the reason why I'm marrying Raul, even though it isn't," Amber said before slamming her hands over her mouth.

"You said more than you meant to," Nora said, stating the obvious again.

Amber nodded her head, her hands still over her mouth.

"I'm sure I'll be able to figure this secret out if I really want to. But if you don't want me to try, I won't. That being said, it might come to me anyway, and I'd much rather hear what's going on from you," Nora said as she patted Amber's knee.

"I know," Amber said, dropping her hands. "I love Raul," she continued as she took hold of Nora's hand.

"I know," Nora responded. It was easy to see that. The adoration in their eyes when Raul and Amber looked at one another would be gag-worthy if it weren't so sweet.

"I've never loved someone like I love him. I want to marry him. The circumstances don't matter," Amber said, her eyes pleading with Nora.

"I believe you," Nora replied.

"We kept everything a secret because he works for us. It seemed so messy, and I was sure it would be a fling, you know? I was new to the island and lonely. It was nice to have someone to talk to other than family. He brought a different perspective. Plus, he's really nice to look at."

"That he is," Nora had to agree.

"But our friendship became more really fast. I could feel I was falling hard, so hard. I woke up every morning thinking about him and he was my last thought before I fell asleep. I thought I was going crazy until Raul told me he felt the same way. I love him so much, Mom," Amber said as she clutched Nora's hand even harder. "By the time I fell for him, it was too late to tell people we were dating and then getting married. Because we have to be married by November if I don't want him to have to leave the country. So we decided to just tell people we were getting married, that we'd been secretly dating and had fallen in love. I would have married him eventually anyway. This is just moving our timeline along."

"His work visa expires?" Nora guessed the secret.

Amber nodded. "I'm the only one who knows because I hired him. We have this complicated system with his last employer so that he could keep the same visa. That's why he goes into Seattle so many days each week. He still bakes for the hotel he used to work at."

Nora had had no idea. Granted, she didn't know Raul very well at all. It was amazing he and Amber had found any time to date. Then again, Amber had been going to Seattle quite a few evenings these past couple of months. This was probably why.

"We needed someone so badly, and Raul wanted to move his

way up in the kitchen. His last job only needed him part-time and were willing to keep all the requirements of his visa. It was kind of a miracle. I didn't know what we'd do in ten months when he had to move, but I figured it would all work out. Either he could get an extension or he'd train a sous chef or he'd have to quit in eight months so that we'd have a buffer of time to find someone new. But then we fell in love and work wasn't the issue at all. Raul would have to leave. And I panicked until I realized the solution was so simple. I would marry him. We'd get married a couple of months before his work visa expires and then he could apply for citizenship."

Amber examined Nora's face as she spoke.

"You think he's using me," Amber said, her voice flat. "He hasn't asked me to do this, you know. He says he wants to marry me whenever I want to get married. That he'd leave if it would make things better. He just wants me to be happy."

"I believe that," Nora said because she really wanted to believe what Amber was saying, and she was pretty sure that she did. It would be hard to be completely sure until she knew Raul better.

Amber breathed a sigh of relief.

"But that does complicate things. Especially because you've known one another for such a short time. I think people will wonder why he can't leave and then come back."

"Because I don't want him to," Amber said, her voice cracking.

Nora pulled her daughter into her embrace. "I know."

"That's why I don't want to tell anyone the truth."

Nora nodded. "I understand. I really do. But that choice comes with a consequence as well."

"Elise," Amber said, seeming to finally realize she had a choice in this as well. She could say a few words and Elise might not be so eager to move. "But she won't understand."

"She might not," Nora agreed.

"And then she'll hate Raul before she even really gets to know him."

"Maybe," Nora said. "But I understand. So she could too."

Amber looked up at Nora, hope in her eyes. "You do?"

Nora wished she could make the decision for Amber and take on the consequences. Amber was stuck between people she loved.

"It's not an easy choice, Amber. I will support you, whatever you decide."

"Thanks, Mom," Amber said, sounding resolute.

Nora had no idea what her daughter would decide, but she knew one thing for sure. She would be true to her word. No matter Amber's decision, she wouldn't be alone.

CHAPTER SEVEN

"DO you think we can have moments of insanity?" Piper asked her therapist.

Dr. Rasmussen sat still, watching Piper for a moment.

"What makes you ask that?" Dr. Rasmussen asked.

Piper shrugged, even though she knew the answer. That dream that hadn't been a dream. Piper was sure Kristie had actually come to her in the night. Her dead daughter had visited her. If anyone understood, it would be her therapist, wouldn't it?

Dr. Rasmussen waited, knowing Piper was holding something back.

"There was a terrible car accident on our island," Piper said instead of answering Dr. Rasmussen's question.

"Was there?" he asked.

Piper nodded. "The woman hurt is the sister of a friend. Fortunately, it seems like she is going to pull through. But tragic things happen. All the time," Piper said, unsure of where she was going. But this suddenly felt important to talk about. Then again, she could just be stalling.

"They do."

Piper cleared her throat. "So what makes my tragedy so

much harder to stomach? I don't think it's imagined. I feel like everyone acknowledges that my heartache is the worst of all. That losing a child is beyond what most can bear."

"Except that you are bearing it."

Piper eyed her doctor skeptically. Was she though? She was maybe losing her mind. She decided it was finally time to reveal what she'd spent her whole session avoiding.

"I had a dream," Piper began, realizing she wanted to be more honest. "Actually, I think it was more than that. I think Kristie visited me. From the other side."

Piper regretted the words the moment she said them aloud. Dr. Rasmussen was definitely the wrong person to say all of this to. The man surely had contacts in mental hospitals all around the United States. And if Piper didn't want to end up in an institution, she needed to at least pretend like she was a whole lot saner.

"Never—" Piper began as Dr. Rasmussen said, "That must have been an incredible experience."

Wait, was he messing with her? Seeing how far Piper would take the charade?

As Piper watched her therapist, she saw nothing but compassion and understanding in his eyes.

"Piper, I see you hesitating. I can understand why. This was the most personal kind of experience you can have. And I would see why you would be scared to share. But I hope that you will. I think that you started to tell me for a reason. So shall we move forward?"

Piper nodded but still couldn't say more.

"You do know that I hear all kinds of things during these sessions. You would be surprised. Even though each case is so unique, there are many similarities between what you are going through and other grieving parents. I've heard a whole lot. And I'll never judge you."

"Even if it sounds like I'm crazy?" Piper asked.

"Especially when it sounds like you're crazy," Dr. Rasmussen returned with a smile.

Piper bit her lip. Could she trust him? She guessed if she couldn't trust him, who could she trust?

"I think she wanted to check on me," Piper finally spoke.

Dr. Rasmussen nodded as if Piper had just told him her favorite flavor of ice cream. Maybe he really had heard it all.

"The whole thing was so strange. In the dream, I knew I'd been missing her, but I wasn't quite sure why. That's why it felt like a dream. Yet the words she said, the way she spoke them. Even as I think about it now, it was like she had learned on the other side and was coming back to impart that knowledge to me. She even looked different. As if she'd grown up since I'd last seen her."

Piper crossed her arms over her chest, feeling vulnerable.

"What did she tell you?" Dr. Rasmussen asked.

A whole lot. Piper would never forget those words. But some of them felt too sacred to ever say to another person. They were special, just for Kristie and Piper. But the core message was what she should tell the doctor. Something he could hopefully help her to accomplish because Piper was stumped.

"She wants me to be happy. She told me loving life again wouldn't mean that I've moved on and left her behind. She said she'll always be with me."

"I know you know that part to be true."

Piper nodded. She did. Kristie was engrained in her soul forever. But the other parts were where Piper was stumped.

"But how can I find happiness?"

Dr. Rasmussen looked up, meeting Piper's eyes.

"If Kristie were the one left here on earth, how would you want her to find happiness?"

Huh. Piper had never thought of that. But it was an easy question to answer.

"Finish school. Find and follow her dreams. Marry the love of her life. Have kids. Love the people she had in her life with such a fierceness that she would forget the ache of losing me," Piper answered quickly.

"So?"

"You think that I can do those things? I'm sorry to break it to you, Doc, but school is something I'll never go back to, I'm too old for dreams, I tried marrying the love of my life and it didn't work out, no husband means no more kids, and there is no way I could ever forget this ache. That I'd ever even want to," Piper said, finally understanding why happiness had been so hard for her to find.

"I'm not sure any of those things are off the table. Except for maybe that last one," Dr. Rasmussen said.

Piper appreciated that the good doctor understood that that last fact was most important, but she still cocked her head skeptically. She was pretty sure all that stuff was off the table, not just the last one. But because he'd recognized that one fact, Piper was ready to give him the benefit of the doubt. At least for a minute.

"Let's focus on this one. Why are you too old for dreams?" he asked.

Piper bit the inside of her cheek as she thought. It wasn't necessarily that she was too old. It was that her dreams had revolved around one person ever since that baby girl had been put in her arms nearly sixteen years ago.

"I guess I'm not too old. More power to anyone who can dream big in their forties. But I had one dream and she died," Piper said, whispering the last word. She surprised herself by not crying. She still ached for her daughter but not for the loss of that dream. She'd come to accept that.

Dr. Rasmussen tapped his pen against his knee. "You know, that's the thing about dreams. I don't think they can die. They can change and adapt, but they are never truly dead."

Piper didn't understand. How could her dream of being a mother to Kristie not have died?

"You are Kristie's mom forever."

Piper nodded. Dr. Rasmussen had explained that before and Piper agreed, but this situation was different. The role was one that now required no work.

"What would you have done when Kristie left the house?" Dr. Rasmussen asked.

Piper didn't know. She'd never thought that far into her dream because Kristie had been so young when her future had been pulled out from under her, so Piper had begun to think of their lives in terms of months instead of years and decades.

"You love photography," Dr. Rasmussen said.

She did. But nothing about that could compare to the role of mother.

She suddenly realized she kind of had thought that far into the future. When Kristie had been really young and Carter had been by her side. All those years ago, when Piper had thought of life after Kristie left the nest, she'd envisioned Carter and herself navigating that road together. Her dreams then had revolved around Carter and Kristie. But when Carter left and Kristie became everything, Piper put her all into her daughter. That couldn't have been healthy, and now she was suffering the repercussions of that choice.

"I think I need an outlet for my love," Piper voiced.

Dr. Rasmussen smiled but didn't say anything.

"How do I find that? I don't want to date." Piper said the last sentence with disgust.

The doctor nodded.

"And I don't feel ready to adopt. I might one day, but if I did it today, I'd be taking in a child to take care of my issues. If I adopt, I want it to be because I have something to offer a child, not the other way around."

Dr. Rasmussen nodded again.

"So what now?" Piper asked. She felt like she'd come to a dead end.

"I think you have a lot to think about," Dr. Rasmussen replied.

That she did. But would thinking help her get answers?

"You have a road map to happiness now, don't you?"

She guessed she did, so Piper nodded. She needed a dream, a cause to put her time into, and a new relationship to nurture— somewhere to put all the love she needed to give. Even just thinking about following through on any of those tasks felt daunting.

But had Piper really expected to leave this session having already found the thing that had been evading her for so long? The doctor was right. The fact that she now knew what she wanted was way more than she'd had in a long time.

With those thoughts, a foreign feeling began to swell in her chest. And Piper realized that for the first time since Kristie had left, she was feeling hope.

CHAPTER EIGHT

"HEY LOU," Marsha murmured sleepily as her sister joined her in the hospital room.

Lou had been visiting every morning since the accident a week before. That night of waiting to hear news about Marsha had been torture. She'd been beaten up badly when the huge truck collided with her car, but the biggest worry had been all her internal bleeding. However, after the initial surgery, doctors had realized things weren't as bad as they'd assumed and were able to stop the bleeding. That had left Marsha with two broken ribs, a couple of black eyes, and a busted lip. A true and complete miracle. There was no other way to explain what had happened. Even the doctors were baffled. That night they'd all been sure that Marsha was on the brink of death. But now she was leaving the hospital tomorrow, just a day over a week from when she'd entered.

"Hiya, Marsha," Lou said with a grin.

"You do realize *hiya* isn't a real word," Marsha said as she shifted in her bed and then groaned. Lou had forgotten to include the many bruises all over Marsha's body when recounting her injuries. But even though those caused discomfort, they were much better than the many broken bones most would have suffered had they endured what Marsha had.

"Yeah, but I figured everyone here is probably being too nice to you. I had to shake it up a bit and annoy you with my use of *hiya,*" Lou said as she took the seat by the head of her sister's bed.

Lou couldn't believe she was joking around with Marsha again. That had to be the even bigger miracle in all of this.

When Marsha had woken up that next morning, her anesthesia had taken a bit to wear off. Lou and Bill had warily made their way into Marsha's hospital room. They were grateful for the good news the doctors had given them but were worried that surly Marsha would have gotten even worse with the tragedy that had befallen her. She had just been told she'd have to stay in the hospital for at least another week, and she was surely in so much pain.

But when Bill and Lou had joined Marsha, they'd been greeted by a soft smile. She'd spoken with kindness and reminded them of the woman she'd once been.

They didn't stay long, and neither Lou nor Bill voiced their shock at the change in Marsha as they left the hospital room that night. But they both knew. This accident had changed something in Marsha.

"You are a brat," Marsha said with laughter as she held her side. "Do you want to know how much it hurts to laugh?"

"Sorry," Lou said quickly, worrying she'd pushed her sister too far. Although Lou was grateful for the changes Marsha was displaying, part of her had to wonder if it was temporary. Would the sister who'd practically hated her return? Lou wanted to just enjoy this time of having her sister back, but it was hard to rely on anything when she had no idea what had brought about this change.

"Don't be sorry. It feels nice to laugh," Marsha said. Then she added, "It's been too long since we've laughed together."

Wasn't that the truth. Marsha and Lou had never been the kind of sisters who were best friends, even though they were barely two years apart. Because their interests had always differed—besides the fact that both had been on the drill team in high school, but Marsha had done it to be cool while Lou had just loved to dance. Marsha had always been very aware of social status while Lou couldn't have cared less, but despite their differences, at the end of the day they knew they were always on the same team. Sure, Marsha had always been a bit more self-involved than Lou would've liked—she'd been a terrible wife to Jared even before her switch in personality—but she'd had other redeeming qualities. She'd been the very best of aunts, spoiling her nieces and nephews as often as she could with not only gifts but time. And even though Lou and Marsha often didn't see eye to eye, when it came down to it, Lou knew Marsha would always be there.

Until their mom had gotten sick. It had all been so quick, it was hard to pinpoint when the change had occurred in Marsha. But Lou just knew it felt like she'd lost her mom and her sister all at once. Marsha was no longer on anyone's side but her own. She still gave Lou's kids elaborate gifts but never spent time with them. It was like someone had snapped their fingers and taken the very best parts of Marsha.

But now she was back. And Lou was going to enjoy her sister for as long as she could. So she shook any worries away and focused on the here and now. Where it felt like Marsha was *her* Marsha again.

"Well, Cash has been teaching me knock knock jokes," Lou replied.

"Oh yeah? Let's hear 'em," Marsha said, trying to sit up in her bed.

Lou jumped up to help her sister and then fluffed the pillows before taking her seat again.

"Knock knock," Lou said with a grin. This was going to be maybe the most terrible joke she'd ever told. But Cash loved it.

"Who's there?" Marsha asked.

"Cow."

"Cow who?"

"Cows moo," Lou replied.

Marsha watched Lou, waiting for more.

"That's it," Lou said.

"Oh my gosh," Marsha said with a chuckle and a shake of her head. "Okay. Give me another one."

"Knock knock."

"Who's there?"

"Lou."

"Lou who?"

"Just Lou. You knocked on my door, remember?"

Marsha began to giggle. "That was so bad."

"Don't let your nephew hear you say that. He made that one up and he's quite proud."

"Really?" Marsha asked, pride filling her voice. "Then it really isn't bad at all."

Lou and Marsha sat in silence for a few minutes. Lou was lost in thoughts about her kids. She really was such a lucky mom. She might've been the very worst at picking a father for her children, but those kids of hers sure made up for it.

Marsha shifted again, causing Lou to look toward her sister.

"Does it hurt?" Lou asked.

"Everything hurts all the time. But I know it could be so much worse. Honestly, it should be so much worse."

Lou nodded. The doctors had told them as much. Lou had really thought she was going to lose her sister for those hours in that dreadful waiting room. Her kids would be losing their aunt, her niece and nephew their mother, her dad his daughter. It was too much for Lou to wrap her mind around, even now that she knew Marsha was okay.

"Cash has grown up so much," Marsha mused.

"He has."

"He's the spitting image of dad at that age," Marsha said.

Lou nodded. Bill loved that since he'd had no sons of his own.

"Lou, be honest with me. Do you think our family still has a spot for me?" Marsha asked.

Lou's stomach dropped. Her sister couldn't be serious. But as Lou met Marsha's eyes, she could see that her sister was completely serious.

"Of course," Lou said, unsure of what more to say. How her sister could ever think that, Lou had no idea.

"It's just, I haven't been around much. I used to hang out with your kids all the time. But now they have Alexis. Dad used to at least need me to come straighten up his place, but now he has Margie for that," Marsha said quietly.

Lou could only imagine what it was taking for her sister to admit these things.

"I miss them," Marsha said as she swiped under her eyes. "I miss you."

Lou's own tears began to fall. She missed her sister. So much. Things hadn't felt right in Lou's life for a long time. Sure, Harvey had made a mess of things, but Marsha being gone had been a huge part of why Lou hadn't felt complete.

Lou opened her mouth to speak when Marsha continued. "I think Mom was with me."

"What?" Lou asked. She wasn't sure where they'd taken a turn in conversation, but she was no longer following.

"In the car. Those moments before the truck collided with me went so slowly. I saw and heard so much in what had to have been a few seconds. I knew that truck was going to hit me and that I would probably die. The people I was going to leave behind ran through my mind. Brittany and Peter." Marsha held her stomach. "I knew I'd miss them so much, but part of me wondered if they wouldn't be better off without me here, holding them back from having a full relationship with their father. I knew what I was doing to them was wrong, having them hold on to hope that we would someday be a family again. But I couldn't lose them. The way I'd lost you and Dad. So I held on with everything I could. I am a terrible, terrible person."

"Marsha—"

"Don't, Lou. I know you think it. Everyone thinks it, and I blame no one for it."

"But Marsha—," Lou tried to say.

Marsha held up her hand, so Lou let it go. For now.

"Then you, dad, Emma, Hazel, Aiden, and Cash filled my thoughts, and I knew it wouldn't matter much to you all either."

"I have to stop you there. You should have seen us in that waiting room, Marsha. We were falling apart. So I can't let you think that for a second longer. Our world would have never been the same without you in it," Lou said forcefully. Marsha had to believe her.

Marsha looked toward her sister, as if gauging the truthfulness of her words.

She must've seen something she liked because she shot Lou a small smile. It wasn't the full blown one that had won Marsha her fair share of beauty titles, but it was a real one. That was what mattered.

"That means everything to me, Lou," Marsha said with a catch in her voice.

Lou nodded, her tears starting again.

Marsha drew in a deep breath. "But even those thoughts

weren't what changed everything for me. As I watched that truck get closer and closer, Mom was there."

Lou's eyes went wide.

"Not physically, like in the sense that you're right here beside me. But I felt like I could see her in my mind's eye. This sounds crazy, doesn't it?"

Lou shook her head. It really didn't. Lou hadn't been to church in years, but she had faith in more than what was here on this earth. She believed these kinds of experiences happened. She just never thought they'd happen to anyone she knew.

Marsha nodded, seeming to appreciate that Lou hadn't called her insane, and continued. "She told me everything was going to be okay. I thought that meant I was going to die. That you all would be okay because I'd no longer be around to add toxicity to your lives."

Lou shook her head, but Marsha ignored her.

"But then she said the words I'd longed to hear for so long. She told me it wasn't my fault."

"What wasn't your fault?" Lou asked, tears streaking her cheeks.

"I . . ." Marsha couldn't seem to get another word out. Her mouth was open but nothing was said.

Lou knew it was imperative that she let Marsha speak. She glanced at the door, hoping no one would enter and break this moment.

"Mom told me months before she got diagnosed that she was worried about the texture around her breast. She'd gone to see a doctor about it and that doctor had said she was fine. I was so relieved to hear those words. Losing mom, I couldn't even imagine it, you know?" Marsha asked.

Lou nodded. That was what had been so hard on all of them. Life without their mother had seemed unfathomable until it happened.

Marsha swallowed. "Mom was still concerned. She wondered if she should get a second opinion. I said . . ." Marsha drew in a deep breath. "I said, 'Why would you do that? You've seen a doctor and gotten a clean bill of health. What would a second opinion do? Besides, who's ever heard of texture under the breast changing as a sign of anything? You're getting older. Didn't those things just happen?' I said enough that Mom didn't get a second opinion. Until two months later. Until it was too late."

Lou's stomach was in knots. She couldn't imagine how Marsha would've felt holding on to that alone for so long.

"I killed Mom," Marsha said, bursting into sobs.

"No, no," Lou repeated, but Marsha didn't hear her. Her shoulders shook as she covered her face with her hands.

Lou put her arm around her sister's shoulders gently. She didn't want to hurt Marsha, but she had to try to offer some sort of comfort.

"Cancer killed Mom," Lou said as Marsha's sobs quieted.

"We could have gotten more treatments. Or at least had more time. I'm the reason she was there one day and gone the next."

That had been exactly what it had felt like. But Marsha couldn't blame herself.

"Marsha, do you even know our parents?" Lou asked.

Marsha tilted her head in confusion as her shoulders still shook with the aftermath of crying so hard.

"Do you think Mom didn't talk to Dad too?" Lou asked.

Marsha bit her lip and then let it go. "Maybe?"

"Not maybe. For sure. Mom and Dad talked through everything that was important. So *they* made the decision. Your words may have factored in, but it wasn't your decision alone. Do you blame either of them for Mom's sudden death?" Lou asked. Lou knew she didn't.

"No," Marsha said slowly. "Although, I have blamed that first doctor. I may or may not have called him to chew him out about it."

Marsha looked ashamed by her actions. Lou wasn't surprised that Marsha had done that during the time after their mom's death. Wait, was this why Marsha had seemed to change overnight as well? She'd held on to this guilt?

Lou asked her sister.

Marsha nodded. "It kept growing every day. I couldn't tell you or dad. I knew it would just hurt you even more while we were mourning the loss of Mom, and then you'd hate me. Other than Brittany and Peter, I quickly realized you two were the only people in the world who'd ever truly loved me. You could never know the truth or I'd lose you. But I couldn't just act the same either. I knew that I was pushing you away with my appalling actions, but it felt like the only way to hold on to my sanity. Then along came Margie and Alexis, seeming to fill every nook and cranny me and mom had filled. You guys didn't need us anymore. You didn't need me."

Maybe it had felt like that was the case to Marsha. Lou could see why. But Marsha had to understand the truth.

"Not only did we need you, we wanted you with us. No one can take the place of family. Even family," Lou said.

Marsha shook her head, seeming too overwhelmed to speak. It was obvious she still had doubts about how much her family wanted her.

Lou's heart ached. How had she not seen that Marsha had only been acting from a place of fear and hurt? Lou realized she'd been pretty consumed by fear and hurt as well. Too much to see outside of her own problems.

Lou gathered her emotions and thoughts, knowing her next words were important. "Marsha, no one could ever replace Mom in our lives. Not even someone as amazing as Margie. I know it's the same for me and Dad because I've talked to Dad about it. Could anyone replace Mom in your life?"

Marsha shook her head.

"So how could you think we could replace you?" Lou asked.

Marsha swallowed and then shrugged. "Alexis seems like the better version of me. And then, not only was she your new sister and Dad's new daughter, she began dating Jared."

"That was my fault," Lou admitted. "Jared had been through so much and he deserved someone who would adore him. I couldn't think of anyone more perfect for him."

"I should've known you were the one who set them up," Marsha said, no true accusation in her voice. "Will she really adore him?" Marsha asked.

"She already does," Lou said quickly.

Marsha nodded.

"But the place Alexis takes in my life and in Dad's life is a new one. It isn't the one that was filled before and left vacant. That spot has stayed vacant in our lives for too long," Lou said.

Marsha's mouth twisted as if she were trying to keep the tears back. She had to know she was fighting a losing battle. Lou felt her own tears return as well.

"So you're telling me there's a chance," Marsha said, quoting one of their favorite silly movies.

Lou burst out laughing. "More of a chance than Jim Carrey had in that moment," she countered with a grin. She stood and leaned over to hug her sister as gently as possible.

"I know I can't repair all that I did or change our past with just this, but I have to say it. I'm so sorry, Lou. I'm sorry I hurt you and that my actions created a rift between us. I'm just so sorry," Marsha said into Lou's shoulder.

Marsha was right that those words wouldn't change the past. But thanks to her sincerity, Lou felt her heart begin to mend immediately.

"You might be wrong again, Sister. I think those words can repair a whole lot," Lou said as she pulled out of the hug. She didn't want to keep leaning on Marsha.

"And all it took was me almost dying. Maybe I should almost die more often."

"Don't even joke about that. I . . . I felt like I was losing part of me that night. I can't go through that again. Don't ever do it again," Lou said.

Marsha nodded. "I'll try. I swear. And I won't joke about it anymore."

"Good."

Lou looked at Marsha and saw her smiling. Marsha, her sister, was actually smiling at her. The moment began to over-whelm her. Lou had stopped dreaming that this could ever be. That she'd have her sister back. She knew there was still a whole lot more to work on. Marsha was right that their relationship couldn't be repaired completely with just that apology, and there was still their dad, Margie, Alexis, Brittany, Peter, Jared, and Lou's kids. But Lou now had hope that they'd get there. And for today, that was enough.

PIPER LAY IN HER BED, cradled in her white comforter as the last vestiges of sleep left her. Kristie hadn't come. Piper had hoped that Kristie coming to her while she slept was the begin-ning of some sort of nightly gift. Or at least a weekly one. But today was the two-week anniversary of that last visit, and Kristie hadn't come again.

She pushed aside the disappointment, remembering the quote, "Don't be sad that it's over. Just be glad that it happened." She was pretty sure she was off by a few words, but the idea worked, especially in this moment. Kristie coming to Piper had changed her life. Or it would as soon as Piper allowed it to.

Awakening also meant focusing on the task her therapist had given her. Piper had avoided it for days now but had promised that after this night, if Kristie didn't come to her telling her otherwise, it meant Dr. Rasmussen was right. And it meant she'd have to really try to start living again. With Kristie in her heart but moving on.

By doing service for someone she loved. After hours of intense thought, Piper had realized that would be the best way to start out on the road map she and Dr. Rasmussen had outlined. She didn't necessarily need a new person in her life to love; she just needed to love those already in her life better.

For now, she was putting the whole dream thing on a back burner. She hoped with time that would come as well, but she just didn't have it in her to dream. And she realized that wasn't a bad thing. Because, like all things, that too would come in time. She just needed to be kind and let herself get there when she could. So until she could reimagine her dreams, Piper was focusing on one thing: loving the people in her life the best she could. Starting with doing service for them.

Piper looked up at the fan on her ceiling. It wasn't moving, so she studied each blade. The grain lines that ran through the fake wood, each one had a purpose. Was Piper like the fan? If she was, Kristie had been those blades. Piper didn't function without Kristie. Or she hadn't. She had been told by not only Dr. Rasmussen, but by Kristie herself, that she had to function without Kristie. There was life in Piper still, even if she despised the situation, so she had to find a way to live. Do more than just survive. Because that's all she'd been doing these past months.

Had it already been nearly half a year? Piper couldn't believe it, but as she did the math, she figured out that, indeed, over five months had been lived since Kristie had left this earth. It just didn't feel right. For the world to keep turning. And yet there was no other way.

Piper realized that in those months, improvements had occurred. She could think about Kristie without bursting into tears. She considered that a win. She was pleased there were now some mornings that she awoke without a headache because she hadn't cried herself to sleep.

And now she was trying to do this. But what was *this* exactly?

Service typically came easily to Piper. She loved seeing the smiles on people's faces after she did something for them. When she thought about service, she came to the conclusion that, honestly, it was a bit selfish because of the high she lived on afterwards. So the actual act of serving wasn't hard. It was the finding who to serve that Piper couldn't quite figure out.

She'd already decided she would do a free photo shoot for a family in need. When she'd told her colleagues at the studio where she worked, they'd quickly jumped on board, loving the idea immediately. They'd told Piper they'd find the family and edit the photos; all she had to do was shoot them. So until they sent her the info, Piper couldn't do anything more on that front.

She'd also talked with her friend, Bess, about working at the local food pantry. Bess had volunteered a whole lot before she'd started her own food truck. Now she was there less often but still did what she could and had connections. When Bess had inquired about how Piper could help, she'd been able to find Piper a shift every Thursday afternoon, starting in October for the duration of the holidays. But because they weren't that busy during their off-season, they didn't need volunteers yet.

And then of course Piper had done random acts of service while she'd been out—helped an older woman carry her groceries to the car, picked up a toy when a child had dropped it —but she didn't feel like this was what she was supposed to be doing. Well, she knew it wasn't. Because the service Dr. Rasmussen had wanted was for someone she loved.

Piper had considered her parents. But they lived far away, and all they really wanted from Piper was for her to start to heal. Piper didn't want to imagine the pain they'd endured, losing their granddaughter and then watching their daughter suffer. So she often tried to hide her anguish from them. She figured maybe that was a service as well?

But she knew that, too, wasn't enough for her therapist and, in the end, for herself. Because even though she was following Dr. Rasmussen's guidelines, she knew they'd only been put in place for her own wellbeing. Doing this would help Piper and Piper alone. Was that why she was having such a hard time following through? She'd never been too great at caring for herself.

But she needed to start doing it. Even if just for Kristie's sake. She had a feeling that as much as her daughter could, Kristie was watching her mother from the other side.

So Piper came back to the name she always landed on. It was his name. Each and every time. She knew what she had to do. He'd been so good to her through all of this, it wasn't like he didn't deserve it. But Piper realized her hesitation had been about more than that. She knew, deep down, that if she served Carter and saw him happy, truly happy, that kind of joy would spread. She would feel it, and then what? She couldn't feel true happiness again, could she? Not without Kristie. And yet that was exactly what Kristie wanted. It was a vicious cycle, and Piper wasn't quite ready to tackle it yet.

But she needed to.

She sat up in her bed too quickly, the room spinning for a moment, before standing up. She walked to her bathroom and began brushing her teeth. It was a Monday, her version of a Saturday. The weekends were always crazy with shoots, but Mondays were usually pretty chill. Like this one. Now that she was only working the forty hours a week she'd promised Dr.

Rasmussen, she had whole days off. Like today. Yet she knew she wouldn't be lazing around in sweats all day.

Because even though she wasn't sure she was ready for this next step, she had to do it. Today. Before she lost her nerve.

This would have been easier to do if Carter was still living down the hall. Knowing Carter, he probably would've suspected something was up even before Piper had known what she was going to do.

But Carter was no longer just down the hall. He'd stayed with Piper for some time after the funeral, long enough for the island gossips to get riled up. But he'd moved out about three months before to the same apartment complex he'd lived in while Kristie had been sick. It had been hard for him to go back, Piper had seen that, but it had made the most sense. Why would he continue to stay with Piper?

His apartment came furnished, so Carter didn't have to worry about outfitting a home. And it was just off of Elliot Drive, making it easily accessible to everything on the island, including Piper's home. It had been close to the hospital as well, but that was no longer a selling point. Because the person they loved was no longer at the hospital . . . .

Piper had to call Carter. Now. Her thoughts had been about to go south, thinking about Kristie—not in the good way, but in the way that would've had her putting away the jeans she was about to pull on and reaching for a pair of sweats instead.

How much would Kristie hate it that she ever brought such an emotion upon her mother? Piper knew if Kristie had her way, her mother would only ever have the best of emotions when thinking about her. So Piper would try to do that for her. One day. And today she'd take a step in that direction. By serving the only person on this earth who had loved Kristie as much as she had. The only person who'd hurt that same way on that day five months ago.

Piper dialed Carter's number and then put her phone on speaker as she washed her face. She'd taken a shower the night before and her hair was still in pretty good shape from when she'd blow dried it. She should probably throw it in a cute updo or something, but all in all, getting ready wouldn't take long. It was early, the best time to invite Carter to join her in one of their favorite pastimes.

Carter was well off. There was no denying that his travel channel and blog had been good to him. He would never have to worry about money, so he had everything he needed and wanted —at least everything he could buy—and Piper knew buying him something wasn't the way he should be served.

Kind words had always meant something to Carter, but composing a text or writing a letter wouldn't mean enough. At least not as much as what Piper had planned.

Quality time. Carter accepted love the best when it came in the form of time together. Well, touch was actually the strongest of Carter's love languages, but Piper wasn't going there. Well, maybe she would give him a hug.

But time together doing the things they loved, that would make Carter's day. Especially doing this specific thing because it had always meant so much to them when they were together. But Piper had been avoiding it because they'd also done it with Kristie. However, it was time.

"Hey, Pipe," Carter answered.

Piper sputtered since she'd just splashed water over her face to wash off the cleanser.

"You okay there?" he asked.

Piper grabbed a towel, drying off her face as she spoke. "Fine. Just washing my face."

Piper didn't dwell on the fact that she wouldn't have called anyone else while doing that task. It was too personal a moment to let most into. But she'd washed her face in front of Carter so many times while they'd been married. Yeah, that was why she hadn't felt weird about calling him now, not that she still felt so close to him.

"So you're fresh and clean?" he asked.

"As good as it's going to get," Piper remarked.

Carter chuckled.

"Are you up to anything today?" Piper asked, a swarm of butterflies filling her belly. Why was she feeling this? It was just Carter. She asked him to do stuff all the time. Strike that. She asked him to do stuff *for her* all the time. This would be *with her*. Completely different. The butterflies in her belly began to throw a freaking party.

"Depends. Why are you asking?" Carter asked.

Couldn't he make this easy on her? The question really should've been answered with a yes or no.

"Because I'm asking. Just answer the question, Carter."

"Feisty. I like it," Carter replied.

Piper grunted.

Carter laughed.

"I have some work stuff I could be doing, but it can be put off if you're asking me because you need me."

Piper's heart leapt. It shouldn't. Carter had said those words so many times before. And not just while they'd been together or while Kristie had been sick. He'd continued saying them up until that day. He'd been there for her. No questions asked. What had she done for him? Nothing. Until now.

"I don't need you."

"Oh."

Piper was sure she heard disappointment in his voice.

"But I'd like to do something with you. If you really have the time. I get it if you need to work or whatever." Piper could feel herself backtracking, but this felt very much like asking Carter on a date. Even though that wasn't what this was. This was service for a man who'd been so good to her. Who'd been hurt just as badly as she had but pushed aside his own hurt to focus on her.

"I'd like to do something with you," Carter said, his voice smoother than it had been before.

Piper's heart flipped again.

Enough of that. This was basically a therapy assignment. There was no need for heart flipping.

"Awesome. I'll pick you up in twenty."

"Okay, see you then," Carter said before ending the call.

Piper breathed in a deep breath, unsure of how she felt. But she had no time to dissect it, considering she had to be at Carter's in twenty minutes.

She put her hands on the counter, letting her head drop. She was going to Carter's. No matter what she told herself, this was kind of like a date. She'd be reenacting what they used to do on their dates. And as much as this was service for Carter, she knew she would enjoy it too. Maybe too much. So much for not dissecting this.

But Carter deserved this.

You deserve it too. Piper thought the words, but she swore they were in Kristie's voice.

Maybe she did?

That was enough time wasted. If she wanted to be out the door in fifteen minutes, she'd better get to work. She needed to apply some makeup and probably pull her hair up. Where they were going, she'd want her hair out of the way.

———

"KRISTIE'S BEACH," Carter said softly as Piper pulled off to the side of the road. This stretch of beach didn't have a parking lot, so Piper had to parallel park. Something she'd never been good at. Fortunately, there were only a few cars parked along the side of the road, so Piper could just drive into a spot.

"Do you remember why we started calling it that?" Piper asked, leaning her head back against the headrest. It was a lot. To be here. With Carter.

Piper had avoided driving past this stretch of beach, much less stopping here or saying the name she associated with this beach.

"Of course," Carter said, interrupting her thoughts. "I still don't get how a kid could hate the beach so much."

Carter chuckled and Piper joined him.

They'd taken Kristie to one of the bigger beaches on the island all the time when she was a toddler. But then on her fourth birthday, they'd all decided to go to the beach for Kristie's birthday. Well, Carter and Piper had. Kristie hadn't been in on the discussions, but she'd always enjoyed the beach before, so Carter and Piper had thought it was the best way to spend the day. Especially because money had been so tight then.

So they'd gone. It was a Saturday. The number of locals and tourists crowding the beach that day had been more than Piper had ever seen before or since. Kristie was hit by a stray frisbee, and it all went downhill from there. The day had ended up with Kristie screaming on her way to the car that she hated the beach. And after that day, she'd refused to go for a whole year.

Until the day that Carter had introduced her to *Kristie's beach*, the same spot he'd taken Piper to all the time back when they'd dated. As soon as Kristie had been let loose on this small stretch of beach, Piper had seen that to Kristie, it felt like this tiny piece of paradise was created just for her.

"I'm not sure what made her love this place. I'd like to think it was more because it was quiet and less because she was narcissistic," Carter teased.

Piper laughed. She'd wondered that as well.

"I'm tired of being sad," Piper said, unsure of why she'd chosen that moment to reveal that thought. But it was the truth. And yet she was scared to no longer be sad.

"Me too," Carter said quietly.

"She would hate it," Piper added. She didn't need to clarify who *she* was. Piper knew the only person who thought about Kristie as often as she did was Carter.

"She would hate this." Carter motioned to the two of them sitting in the car as the beach beckoned.

"Let's get out there, Mom." Piper gave her best impression of Kristie.

Carter laughed. "She was so much like you."

"She had the best parts of both of us."

Carter nodded and then looked at Piper. "So do we listen to her?"

"Don't we have to?" Piper asked.

Carter nodded again before getting out of the car and rounding it so that he could open Piper's door. He stood, with the door open. All Piper had to do was step out.

So she did.

But there was one more thing she had to do. Something she wasn't sure she could do. She drew in a deep breath of sea air, letting that buoy her.

"We need to try to make this a happy outing," Piper said. She swore she heard Kristie laugh. Why would anyone have to try to make the beach happy, she would've asked. This coming from the girl who'd screamed her way away from the beach. Granted, she'd only been four then, and she'd since proven how much she loved this place.

"I can do that," Carter said.

"Happy thoughts, happy memories, and happy moments."

"I like it." Carter smiled.

Piper thought she did too. Even though it felt a bit disloyal.

Piper stepped to the back of the car. "So, speaking of happy memories . . ." She opened the trunk and pulled out a brown paper bag with a yellow M emblazoned on it. She hadn't eaten at this place in years, but it was all she and Carter had ever eaten for breakfast when they'd come to the beach back when they were dating.

"I thought I smelled a sausage biscuit!" Carter exclaimed as he saw the bag.

Piper had put the food in the trunk the moment she'd gotten it to keep the smell from infiltrating the whole car. She'd wanted to keep it a surprise.

She handed the bag to Carter. He held it in one hand and then glanced down at the hand that had just given him the food: Piper's hand. Then he glanced back to his free one.

Her heart squeezed. Didn't it get the memo that this was a no-heart-squeezing zone? But it wasn't listening. With the way the intense look on Carter's handsome face was affecting the rest of her, Piper couldn't blame it.

Carter met her eyes, and she knew what he was asking. She gave the tiniest nod, and he smiled before letting his strong, long fingers embrace her own.

Butterflies were now joining her squeezing heart, and Piper knew she was fighting a losing battle. Might as well give in.

So she smiled as Carter led her along the beach.

"Close to the rock?" Piper asked.

Carter nodded. A huge rock sat in the ocean just off the beach. It was where they'd always sat during their dates. Their family moments had been spread out all over the beach—Kristie had always chosen their spot—but today it felt right to go back to their place.

They stopped walking, and Carter handed the bag back to Piper as he looked to the ground and saw they'd be sitting on bare sand.

"Don't you dare," Piper said, knowing exactly what he was doing. "I should have brought a blanket," she added. She couldn't believe she'd forgotten a dang blanket.

"But you didn't. So now you have to take my shirt."

Carter had done the same thing on their very first date to the beach. Well, almost. He'd been the one to forget a blanket then, so he'd taken off his jacket, even though it was February and so cold that they'd only lasted for a few minutes on the beach. But it had been in that moment, when Carter had sacrificed his jacket, that Piper had known this was going to be a man in her life for a long time. And somehow, he was still here . . . a marriage, a child, a divorce, and a lost child later.

"Is this my punishment?" Piper asked as Carter began to unbutton his shirt. Having to take Carter's shirt would be embarrassing, to say the least. She should've been more prepared.

Carter laughed. "Don't worry, I'm wearing a shirt under this one."

Piper knew he was. She hadn't forgotten Carter's dressing habits. He liked having an undershirt on under all of his button ups.

"Seeing you without a shirt on isn't exactly a punishment," Piper said before slapping a hand over her mouth. She had *not* meant to say that.

Carter burst into laughter as Piper's cheeks turned a bright red.

Carter began unbuttoning his shirt, and Piper would've continued to fight him that she could just sit on the sand if she weren't so busy being mortified.

"Good to know I've still got it," Carter said as he lay his shirt on the ground and then motioned for Piper to sit.

Piper shook her head, but she couldn't deny it. Despite their hard times and divorce, Piper had never quit being attracted to her ex. She probably never would.

"And Pipe?" Carter said as Piper sat and he plopped down beside her. "You've still got it too."

Cheeks flaming, butterflies rioting, and heart squeezing combined. Piper hadn't felt this happy in so long. And it felt good.

But what about Kristie?

Whether it was her own mind or really Kristie saying the words, Piper would never know. But her guilt lifted as she heard the words, *Just enjoy it, Mom. I am.* Piper swore she heard Kristie's laughter get swept away by the wind.

Kristie and Dr. Rasmussen were right. Moving on didn't mean leaving Kristie behind. She was here. The way she'd always been and always would be.

CHAPTER NINE

JULIA'S KNEE bounced as Ellis drove them onto the ferry. At a bump on the ramp, her knee hit the dashboard, causing a word she hadn't said in years to pop out of her mouth.

Ellis glanced over, concern written all over his features.

"You okay?" he asked.

Julia nodded as she rubbed her knee. She must have hit her funny bone because, even though it had really hurt, she doubted it would even bruise.

At Julia's nod, Ellis's face took on a grin. "And what was it that you just said?" he teased.

"I can't believe I said that," she replied. All the pain which she'd felt was now completely gone, leaving just humiliation behind.

"It was hilarious," Ellis assured as he put the car in park, then put his arm around Julia and pulled her in.

"I thought my days of swearing were behind me, but I guess all I need is to feel a little nervousness and they bubble right back out," Julia said, leaning into Ellis's strength.

She could have managed picking Wendy up all on her own, but she was grateful she didn't have to. It was nice to have a person beside her that she could truly count on. She'd had assistants and other people in her camp who were supposed to be supports for her, but Julia had always found something lacking. After being with Ellis, she realized what it was. True loyalty. Those people had been paid to help Julia; Ellis did it because he loved her. That was pretty powerful.

"Are you nervous?" Ellis asked, kissing the top of Julia's head. Heavens, she could stay like this forever.

"Do spiders jump?" Julia asked, her mind not really in their conversation. She was too busy enjoying the feel of Ellis loving her, and she also couldn't remember if she'd left a razor in Wendy's bathroom or not. She'd tried to outfit the room and bathroom her niece would be in with everything the girl could possibly need. Julia knew she'd bought an extra razor to put in Wendy's bathroom, but she couldn't for the life of her remember if she'd taken it into that bathroom after the grocery order had arrived.

Along with making sure the room and bathroom were stocked, Julia had stocked her kitchen with every one of Wendy's favorite foods. The list had been a little hard to get since Lacey was against all of this, but Julia's mom had come through with all they needed. Julia now had Fruit Loops and two-percent milk in her kitchen for the first time ever.

"Well, some of them do," Ellis replied.

Julia scanned her brain. What had they been talking about? Oh right, jumping spiders. Her analogy had been terrible—she'd forgotten that not all spiders jump—but she was going to go with it.

"And this Julia is nervous," Julia said, causing Ellis to chuckle.

"What is going on in that magnificent mind of yours?" Ellis murmured against Julia's hair.

If only Ellis knew, he would probably think her mind a

whole lot less magnificent. But since he'd asked. "Do you know if I put the razor in Wendy's bathroom? I bought her one, and I don't want to go in there after she gets to the house. I want her to know that the whole area is her domain and I won't impose," Julia said, tapping her fingers against her jean-clad leg. She hadn't tapped her fingers like this since she'd been waiting to hear if she'd won her second Academy Award. She had. In case anyone was keeping track. But that was to say Julia was probably more than a little bit on edge. Why was she this ball of nerves? It was just her niece coming for a visit.

"That's really nice of you. But one, I'm pretty sure Wendy will bring her own razor. Didn't you have like six boxes worth of her stuff show up last week? She's moving out here. If she needs a razor, she probably already owns one. And two, you could always hand it to her later. In the hall. In the public domain," Ellis teased again.

Julia smiled, ease relaxing the knot that had been in her chest. Ellis was so good at that.

"You're right," she said with a sigh.

"I usually am," he replied.

Julia laughed as she tickled Ellis's side. He yelped and moved to the other side of the car. Figuring out Ellis was ticklish just in that one spot was one of Julia's greatest accomplishments. She now finally had a way to get him back after he teased her.

"And now I feel like I can't be vulnerable with you," Ellis joked.

Julia rolled her eyes, and Ellis laughed as he went right back to where he'd originally been. Holding Julia next to him.

"Do you really think she'll like it?" Julia asked.

"That bedroom/bathroom combo would be any woman's dream," Ellis said knowingly.

"How would you know?"

"I've been known to dabble on Pinterest," he admitted.

"You don't," Julia squealed.

"I don't if anyone besides you asks. But yeah, it's kind of soothing," he said.

Julia laughed. Her man was full of surprises and she loved it.

"And in the tiniest of chances that she doesn't, it will be okay. I know this is the first time family has ever visited your home, but you need to relax. That will matter to Wendy much more than a razor," Ellis reassured.

Wait, was this the first time family had ever visited her? It seemed almost unbelievable, but she realized it was. There'd been the too many years that she'd been estranged from them, and after that, she'd always gone back to Travers. No one had ever come to any of her homes. Now her mounting anxiety made perfect sense.

"Thank you, Ellis," Julia said, kissing his cheek because she knew if she went for his lips, she wouldn't be able to draw away as quickly.

Even though Whisling's residents had gotten used to the celebrity couple being in their midst, she knew that if someone were to catch them kissing in public, it might be too much of a temptation for them to take a video and sell it to the highest bidder. And then the tranquil life they'd created on the island would be gone. They'd be back to being the movie star and country star who'd found love against a quaint backdrop. The paparazzi would surely swarm them if there was any story to be found. Right now they were so boring that no one cared to go out of their way to photograph them. And Julia needed to keep it that way. Even if she wanted nothing more than to make out with her boyfriend.

Julia's phone started ringing, cutting off her thoughts.

The name on the caller ID stunned her. Even though Julia

had Lacey's contact information saved in her phone, she never thought her sister would actually call her.

"Are you going to answer it?" Ellis asked when Julia had sat staring at her phone for too long.

Julia nodded before pressing the green button to answer and then putting the call on speaker phone. Because they were in Ellis's car and not her own, her phone didn't automatically connect to the car's sound system.

"Really, Julia? This is how you repay me?" Lacey said before Julia even had the chance to say hello.

Repay her? Julia was lost, and the conversation had just started. This didn't bode well for her, especially considering Lacey's tone. Her sister was even more unhappy than when she typically spoke to Julia. And that was saying something.

"Hi, Lacey." Julia shot for being cordial. Maybe her sister would follow her example?

"Don't *hi Lacey* me. You should have told her to stay home. Where she belongs," Lacey spat.

This was about Wendy. Of course it was. Julia should've known. But she'd been so surprised to see Lacey's name on her caller ID that all rational thought had fled.

But this made sense. Lacey was upset. Julia knew she would be. She just never thought Lacey would voice any of that to her. Lacey seemed perfectly content ignoring Julia forever. But now Lacey was leveling accusations. Telling Julia what she should have done. Had Lacey really expected Julia not to accept her niece into her home?

"I couldn't do that, Lacey."

"Yes you could have and you should have," Lacey demanded. "You know what you leaving did to our family. You tore us apart. I won't let you do this to my family as well."

Julia literally bit on her lip to keep from retorting. The rift in their family had not been one-sided. In fact, Julia was doing all she could to bridge that gulf. Lacey was the one who was holding on to her grudge and wouldn't forgive her sister. But Julia said none of that, trying to focus on the important person in all of this. Wendy.

"She wanted to move somewhere new. That isn't a crime, Lacey."

"No doubt because of your influence. My Wendy was more than content to make her home here forever until you showed up."

Julia again tried to ignore the underlying implications. Lacey was practically telling Julia she wished she'd stayed away forever.

Ellis's arm around her tightened and he kissed her head again, reminding Julia she wasn't alone.

Thank heavens.

"I don't know if I'm the reason she chose to move. But I can promise you, Lacey, I said nothing to her about it. That was all from her. And it doesn't have to be so bad. If Wendy saw that you—"

"Are you really trying to give me parenting advice? You, a woman whose greatest accomplishment is pretending to be other people, think you can tell me, a woman who has been a mother for over two decades, how to parent?" Lacey asked, each word cutting. Not only had Lacey reminded Julia that she didn't have a family of her own, not in the traditional sense at least, she'd minimized everything Julia had worked so hard to accomplish into something that felt childish at best, ridiculous at worst.

Julia felt tears sting her eyes. She wasn't surprised that Lacey was lashing out, but this was too much.

"You can hang up, Darlin'," Ellis whispered into her ear.

She could. And she was going to. The last couple of years, Julia had done everything she could to try opening a path for a relationship with her sister. But Lacey had never reciprocated. Maybe Julia had done too much. Maybe her actions told her sister it was okay to treat her like this. But now she was going to let Lacey know that wasn't the case.

"You don't know—" Lacey began again, but Julia was done.

She gathered every ounce of her strength, cleared her throat and said, "Good bye, Lacey," before hanging up the phone.

Julia stared down at the device. Lacey was gone. Because Julia had pressed the end call button. Long before Lacey was ready.

Julia turned her wide eyes to Ellis.

"She deserved at least that. I was ready to give her the tongue lashing of a lifetime. It was better you ended the call," Ellis assured.

But was it? Lacey would only be more upset, and any ground Julia had gained with her sister was gone. Granted, she hadn't gained much ground with her sister anyway. Maybe this was really for the best?

The phone began ringing again. Julia didn't have to look to know who was calling.

"Do you think she's going to apologize?" Ellis asked.

"Is the sun yellow?" Julia asked.

Ellis cocked his head as he considered the question. "It typically is, but in certain lights—" Ellis said, and Julia realized this analogy was worse than her last. Because what she'd meant was *no*. There was no way in heck Lacey was going to apologize.

"No," Julia said, cutting off Ellis.

"*No* she's not going to apologize?"

"Not a chance."

"Then you probably shouldn't answer."

Julia knew Ellis was right, so she handed him the phone. She'd be too tempted to answer without some type of barrier keeping her from the phone.

Ellis's car stayed silent as they docked in Seattle and then drove off the ferry. It wasn't until they neared the airport that Ellis spoke again.

"You know nothing she said was true, right?" he asked, placing a comforting hand on Julia's thigh.

"I'm not a parent."

"That doesn't mean you're wrong."

Julia guessed that was true. But the hollowness that filled her chest every time she thought about the fact that she was childless had practically taken over.

Julia tried to swallow back the discomfort, but it remained. She wouldn't change her past. Everything she'd done in her life had brought her right here. But part of Julia wondered what it would have been like. To stay in Travers and have the family her mom had wanted for her. Or to have moved to LA and concentrated a bit of her effort on dating instead of just her career. Would she have found Mr. Right?

Considering the only man in the world who could have ever filled that role was sitting beside her now, post-career, she figured that probably wouldn't have been the case. Julia had been destined for the movies. It was the life she'd been born to live. But it had come with sacrifices, children being one of them. She knew she could adopt now but, honestly, she felt too old to just be entering that phase of life. Julia realized that deep down she'd hoped having Wendy here would kind of fill that hole. And that was why Lacey's call had hurt so much. The reminder that any role Julia played in Wendy's life other than aunt would be like another part in a movie. She'd be pretending. That was it. And that hurt more than Julia cared to admit.

"I think it just hit me harder than ever that I made the choice to do something besides be a mom. I sacrificed that role for the others I wanted," Julia said as they drove into the terminal. She started keeping her eyes peeled for the airline Wendy was flying.

"Do you wish you'd done it differently?" Ellis asked softly.

Julia knew she didn't. "I think I wish I could have had both."

"Now that's just a little greedy, isn't it?" Ellis teased.

Julia laughed. It was. But that didn't stop her from wishing.

"Did you have a relationship where you considered having children?" Ellis asked.

Heck to the no. None of the men Julia dated in Hollywood were dad material.

"I'm guessing by your wide eyes that the answer is no."

Julia nodded.

"If you had forced children into those relationships, what would that have done?"

Julia hadn't thought of that. Those kids would be so messed up. Julia had had a hard enough time taking care of herself. Being enough for herself. She'd been too wrapped up in her own problems to be what a child needed.

"Why do you always have to be right?" Julia asked.

"It really is a gift," Ellis drawled.

Julia smiled. What would she do without this man? He'd done that twice in one day now. Julia still felt a longing for children, but now she didn't resent being childless. And maybe one day she'd come to accept it. Because Ellis was right. Her life hadn't been equipped to do anything more. Julia was in a great place now, but for so much of her life she hadn't been. If she'd been parenting during those times? Thank goodness she hadn't subjected a child to such a life. For that, she kind of felt proud.

"Oh, it's that one," Julia said.

Ellis pulled to the curb, and they looked one way, then the other.

"Has her flight landed?" he asked.

Oh. Right. Julia had meant to check that.

She opened her phone to find the app of the airline and saw that Wendy's flight had just landed. Meaning there was no way she could already be at the curb.

As Julia's phone was open, Wendy texted, *Just landed. See you soon!*

"I think it might still be a few minutes?" Julia said.

Ellis chuckled as he pulled away from the curb and began to drive, this time a little more slowly.

"So are you really feeling alright? We experienced a few ups and downs on this car ride," Ellis said, kindly including himself in the rollercoaster ride Julia's emotions had just experienced.

"I am. For now. Though you might have to talk me off another ledge in about fifteen minutes." Julia grinned but she was kind of serious.

"Always Darlin'," Ellis said, returning Julia's grin.

"OH IT'S BEAUTIFUL, AUNT JULIA," Wendy gushed as Julia guided her to her bedroom. Julia had even snuck a peek into the bathroom and seen that there was, indeed, a razor.

Wendy's gaze bounced around the room, first taking in the bed clad with a gray comforter and a white blanket stretched across the bottom. Gray and white pillows sat against a tufted gray headboard. Julia had found a fluffy white bench to put at the bottom of the bed, matching the ghost white of the walls and the sheer curtains. A simple silver chandelier hung from the dark wood planks that Julia had had a contractor put on the ceiling. A dresser made of the same wood as the ceiling sat against a wall with a gigantic mirror over it.

"Is it too chic?" Julia worried. Her decorating style seemed to drive her in just one direction. Chic. And she'd been told by numerous ex-boyfriends that she went overboard.

"Too chic? Is there such a thing? No, it's perfect," Wendy gushed as she set her suitcases near the door. "But I am a little worried I'm too much of a mess for this much white." She looked down at the plush white carpet. "Luckily, I'll only be here a few days."

"What?" Julia asked. This was news to her.

"I know you said I could stay here as long as I needed, and I really appreciate that, but I'm trying to keep what I need to a minimum. I have an appointment with a realtor to look at apartments tomorrow. I'll be starting my new job on Monday, and I have inquiries out for some cars that I'm interested in," Wendy shared, explaining her plans in basically one breath.

Julia tried not to look shocked. She hadn't been expecting Wendy to be so prepared to be on her own. But she was proud of her niece. "I do need to ask you a favor though," Wendy added.

"Anything," Julia promised. She'd anticipated having Wendy in her home for much longer, but she needed to follow the advice she'd tried to give Lacey. They needed to let Wendy fly. And man, was she soaring.

"Do you know a mechanic on the island that I can trust? The cars I'm looking at are used, so I'd like someone to look at them before I decide which one to buy."

That felt too simple a request. Did Wendy have the money she needed for all of this? A car *and* a deposit for an apartment? That would be a lot of cash for any twenty-something to have on hand.

"One, that isn't a favor; it's a given. And two, Ellis knows his way around anything that drives. He'd be totally capable of looking over cars for you."

"Thank you," Wendy gushed.

She was grateful for too little.

"But will that stretch you? A car and a deposit?" Julia asked cautiously. She didn't want to imply Wendy couldn't take care of it all on her own, but she knew her niece couldn't have been making much at the bank back in Travers.

"I lived at home, remember? And I'm a saver. I think I knew I'd want to do something like this one day and would need a nest egg. I've got it covered. But thank you for caring, Aunt Julia," Wendy said, completely unlike her mother.

Julia needed to stop anticipating Lacey when she interacted with Wendy. But it was hard, considering Wendy was the spitting image of her mother. From the long, dark hair to the light blue eyes. Their curvy body types were even similar. Ellis was going to need to step up his uncle game while Wendy was here. Julia wondered if Ellis had a shotgun he could be cleaning when Wendy's dates came to pick her up.

"You're lost in thought," Wendy said.

Julia nodded. "Sorry about that. I was just wondering if Ellis owned a shotgun."

"Does he need that to check out cars?" Wendy asked, an eyebrow raised.

"Oh no. You're just so gorgeous. I have a feeling he'll need to fend off a few losers," Julia said.

Wendy laughed. "I do tend to attract a lot of them."

Julia had put her foot in it, and she immediately felt the need to apologize. "I'm sorry, I didn't mean to imply that you only attract losers."

"No offense taken. How can I be offended in a place like this?" Wendy twirled around in the room and then walked to the window, which had a perfect view of the ocean.

What a delight to be around someone so easy and breezy. Julia gave in to her urge to tease. "Glad to know. I'll be sure to say everything on my mind then," she joked.

Wendy laughed again. Julia loved that sound.

"So Ellis doesn't live with you?" Wendy asked since Ellis had dropped the two of them off and said he was going home.

"No. Not until he puts a ring on it."

Wendy laughed harder at Julia's dated pop culture reference.

"I guess I'm getting old-fashioned in my old age," Julia added, feeling the need to explain her decision.

Wendy's laughter stopped abruptly. "You are not old, Aunt Julia."

Julia grinned at Wendy. Her niece was being too kind, considering their thirty-year age gap. But Julia would take the compliment.

"So apartment shopping tomorrow. When were you planning on looking at cars?" Julia asked, taking a step back. She should probably leave Wendy alone soon, but she was truly enjoying her company so it was hard to.

"Hopefully tonight? Is there a bus system on the island? I have the addresses of the people selling their cars. Maybe Ellis could meet me at the couple of spots if it isn't too much to ask," Wendy said, grimacing with worry that she was overstepping.

"Wendy. You are asking for practically nothing. And there is a bus system, but you will not be taking it. We can drive to Ellis's and grab him before heading to these unknown persons' houses. Like I would let you go to some stranger's house alone," Julia said, mumbling the last sentence.

Wendy grinned. "Mom was telling me I would be an inconvenience to you, and I just want to keep from doing that. I'm thrilled to be living close to you, so I don't want to hurt our relationship before it starts," Wendy admitted, her grin disappearing.

"I was planning on having you live with me for the duration of your stay here. I was also hoping to be able to buy you a car. I wanted to spoil my one niece, so you are definitely not at all an inconvenience. But I understand that I need to let you gain your independence."

Wendy's grin was back.

"So let's agree to this. You lean on me a bit more, and I'll try to let you live your own life as much as I can."

"Sounds good to me. And I'm always okay with a little spoiling," Wendy agreed with a twinkle in her eye.

Julia laughed. She was going to look forward to that spoiling. She'd always wanted to lavish gifts on her nephews and niece but knew her siblings wouldn't appreciate that. Now that Wendy was close, Julia was going to pounce on the opportunity. Looking at Wendy, Julia was again reminded how beautiful her niece was. She had promised her space, but there was one aspect of life she'd need to encroach just a bit.

"Oh, except when you're going on dates. Then Ellis and I will be waiting on your front porch cleaning our shot guns."

Wendy burst into laughter.

Julia had a feeling she was really going to enjoy this phase of her life.

CHAPTER TEN

ALEXIS HAD NEVER UNDERSTOOD the term *a stomach in knots* until this very moment. Her insides felt twisted in a way they'd never felt before, but she had to continue forward.

She'd parked her car in the small parking lot beside the condo complex where Marsha resided.

Yes, she was meeting up with Marsha. A plan they'd made of their own accords. Marsha, the woman who'd done her very best to tear the person Alexis loved most in the world away from her, had invited Alexis to her home. And Alexis was going.

Lou was full of hope. It was a beautiful sight to see. Her best friend who'd lost her mother and husband and what felt like her sister, all within a year, was now hopeful again. And it was all to do with the woman sitting just a few stories above where Alexis stood.

Lou had told her that Marsha had changed. She was trying to mend wrongs she'd committed against Lou, not just by word but by deed. Even though Marsha was still a little battered from her accident, she'd babysat for Lou—which was basically akin to giving an organ, in Lou's book. She adored anyone who was willing to take on all four of her kids at once.

According to Lou, Marsha loved the experience and wanted to do it again soon. Marsha had also spent most of the last week since she'd gotten out of the hospital with her own children, asking Jared if the kids could spend an extra night with her because they were having so much fun just watching movies and playing games. That alone gave Alexis pause. Marsha spending an evening doing things that didn't cost a ton of money and enjoying it? It sounded fantastical, to say the least.

But fantastical seemed to be the right word to describe all the changes in Marsha. She'd even invited Margie and Bill over for lunch, ordering the food for their meal and then somehow cleaning it up after they left . . . with two broken ribs.

Basically, it felt like Marsha was accomplishing the impossible. And now she'd texted Alexis asking her if there was a time they could meet up.

Alexis couldn't lie. For a moment she was sure it was some sort of prank. Right out of a teen movie. It had to be a set-up, right?

But then she'd told Lou who was sure this meant that Marsha was regretting the time she'd spent pushing Alexis away. Now they would all three not just be sisters by happenstance but best friends by choice. Alexis had laughed at that prediction, and even Lou understood it was a bit much to hope for the *best friends* part. It would take an act of God for that to happen.

Alexis wasn't holding her breath about her relationship with Marsha changing, but she was trying to be optimistic because Lou was right about Marsha making so many changes. And Alexis was all for Lou forgiving her sister, if that was what she wanted to do. But Alexis was more than a little worried for everyone involved. What if this was a temporary change? It seemed too genuine to just be an act—Alexis would give Marsha that—but what if Marsha changed her ways tomorrow, going back to the way she'd always been?

Although, according to Lou, Marsha hadn't always been the way she was. Lou had said some things were too personal to Marsha for Lou to share, but they'd been through a lot with the death of their mother and it had changed Marsha to the person she'd been since Alexis had known them. Marsha of yore had always been a bit self-centered but nothing like the woman she'd been these past few years, at least according to Lou.

So Alexis was trusting Lou. Which was why she about to take an elevator up four flights to talk to Marsha. Right now.

Looking at the building, Alexis remembered a conversation she'd had with Jared months before. When Marsha had moved out of his house, she had insisted she could only move into a penthouse. Alexis wasn't sure that this fourth story condo could be considered a penthouse, but apparently it had appeased Marsha.

So how could that woman, the one who hadn't cared where or how Jared got the money for her new condo, be this same woman who Lou was describing now? It had been the penthouse or bust, even when Jared had explained that he couldn't afford the condo Marsha wanted as well as their family home. Unless he pulled Peter and Brittany out of some activities. The very lessons that Marsha had insisted the kids take. But she hadn't cared. She'd been fine with taking from her own children to have the housing set up she desired. This was the same woman who was now babysitting for free and putting her kids' needs first? Alexis couldn't help but feel a little skeptical. Sure, people had come-to-Jesus moments when they came close to death, but were they this drastic? And if they were, did they last?

Alexis had a feeling she was about to find out. This meeting would be Marsha's greatest test of her newfound repentance.

Would she feel any remorse for the way she'd treated Alexis? Or, more importantly, what she'd done to her own children? Making Brittany and Peter think that the only thing in the way of all their happily-ever-afters was the evil Alexis. Making them hope for a future where their mom and dad would be together, even though she knew full well it would never be. Because Marsha hadn't wanted it. She'd only wanted her kids to think that she wanted it. It had been cruel.

Although, according to Jared, Marsha had already told her kids the truth about that one. During one of their sleepovers, she'd sat them down and apologized. She'd said that mom and dad loved them so much but were better apart. They could still be a family, but it would look different than the family they'd been in the past. Marsha had said all the right things to her kids, things she should've said long before, and Alexis had to give her credit. Even if it was months too late.

But now what? What would Marsha say to Alexis? Alexis had tried for a long time to be a friend to Marsha but was now not just wary. She thought about how she might not want a relationship with the woman, even if Marsha offered one.

Would she offer one? That felt extreme, but nothing Marsha was doing was in character.

Alexis decided worrying was just borrowing trouble. She couldn't predict what Marsha was going to do because nothing Marsha had been doing had been predictable. So she would just drive herself crazy trying to figure out what was coming.

But what she did need to do was get up there and get this over with. That was the only way she'd know why Marsha wanted to speak to her.

So Alexis quieted her thoughts as she rode the elevator to the fourth floor and stepped out, reading the numbers next to the doors. Marsha was in four-oh-three.

The beige walls matched the beige carpet. A runner of blue

and gold ran down the middle, giving the place a regal flair she was sure Marsha loved. The bright white doors were a strong contrast to the colors in the rest of the hall, and Alexis walked past two of those doors before reaching her destination.

She was here. Deep breath in and out.

She swallowed, her frustration with Marsha suddenly leaking out of her now at the last minute. She was supposed to hold on to that. That would be her shield in case Marsha wasn't kind. In case this was all just a prank. In case Marsha wanted everyone else in her life but was still going to push Alexis away.

Alexis put a hand to her chest, massaging away the ache. It hurt that it had taken Marsha so long to reach out to her. Everyone else had received apologies within the first two days after she'd been discharged from the hospital or, in Lou's case, at the hospital. But now, five days later, here Alexis stood. Not knowing how Marsha truly felt about her.

Their interactions had been few. Most of what Alexis knew about Marsha was secondhand. And yet she was judging her. Then again, hadn't Marsha judged Alexis? It was only fair that Alexis did the same. But Alexis didn't typically err on the side of just fair. She tried to be kinder than the treatment she was given. For some reason with Marsha, that had felt like an impossibility.

But Alexis was here. She was going to walk in, be brave, find out what Marsha wanted, and then she would leave. Back to her own home. Back to people who loved her. No matter what Marsha said, it wouldn't change who Alexis was.

But Alexis had never been despised before. Not like this. It was new territory. And she hated it. Especially because, technically, she and Marsha were now family. If Alexis was really being honest with herself, she hoped beyond hope that Marsha would raise a white flag and the two could at least be cordial. Heck, because all of Alexis's angry words were really just a facade protecting her hurt, Alexis would take a cream-colored flag at this point. As long as it resembled a truce, Alexis would take it.

Alexis raised her hand to knock on the door.

One, two, three knocks. What was a polite number of knocks? Had Alexis done too many? Too few?

Oh goodness, she missed fake-angry Alexis who could at least pretend that she didn't care what Marsha thought.

The door opened and there stood Marsha, the nicest expression she'd ever worn in Alexis's presence on her face. But that wasn't saying much considering she'd pretty much only ever been livid in front of Alexis. The expression she wore now was pretty neutral, but Alexis would take it.

Moving beyond the expression, Alexis really took Marsha in. She was wearing joggers—probably because actual waistbands were hard on her ribs—which was shocking considering even casual Marsha used to wear dress pants. She wore a blouse tucked into the joggers—not quite fashionable, yet on Marsha it worked. Her typically blonde, curled hair fell straight around her face, and her roots were grown out a bit, making Alexis wonder how often Marsha usually dyed her hair. The accident had only happened a little over two weeks ago.

"You came," Marsha said.

Again, no emotion. But Alexis would take that over hostility.

"I did," Alexis said, wiping her sweaty hands on the back of her blue jeans. Unlike Marsha, she'd dressed up for the occasion. Alexis wore jeans, a flowy striped blouse, and her favorite cream-colored sandals.

Marsha pushed the door open and then walked away. Alexis guessed that meant she should enter?

So she did, closing the door behind her. She walked a few uneasy steps, hating that she felt like she'd just walked into the lair of the evil villain. But then again, Marsha had never tried to be anyone else in the story of Alexis's life.

Marsha sank down on her couch, and Alexis caught a glimpse of pain on Marsha's face before her neutral expression came right back into place. Had she practiced that look before Alexis had come over? Because she was really good at it.

"I've never liked you," Marsha said from her spot on the couch as Alexis stood awkwardly in the middle of the room since she hadn't been offered a seat.

Wow. That was one way to start a conversation. Not a good way, but a way.

Alexis stuck her hands in the back pockets of her pants, trying to find a casual way to stand in the middle of a foreign room.

"Even before all of the Jared stuff. When you were just my soon-to-be stepsister."

Okay. Alexis got it. Marsha always hated her. Great. Now could she go?

Alexis shifted so that her weight was evenly distributed between her feet. She was ready to walk out. She should've known to never get her hopes up.

Alexis cracked her neck as she waited. Was Marsha done? Couldn't this have been said over text? Maybe even an email? A Facetime call if she'd wanted to see Alexis's reaction?

"Are you going to say anything?" Marsha asked.

"I'm not sure what I'm supposed to say to that," Alexis admitted.

"Always the nice girl. Miss goody two-shoes personified," Marsha muttered. "Say how you felt about me," she added, those words crystal clear.

Alexis narrowed her eyes at the woman who sat in front of her, no sign of a flag, white or otherwise, in sight. Did Marsha really want to do this? Alright. But only because she'd asked for it. And because she'd insulted Alexis. The impact of those words were still smarting. If Marsha wanted honest, Alexis could do honest.

"I thought you were spoiled at best. And that was before I met Jared and your wonderful children."

"Right," Marsha said, but Alexis wasn't done.

"You had the greatest people in the world all fighting to love you, and you pushed every one of them away. Bill is the best of men, but you said words to him that I wouldn't have spoken to the vilest of creatures. The man who raised you, who did nothing but love you. And then Lou." Alexis shook her head. "Lou has the biggest heart in the world. One that was broken once by your mother on accident and so many times by Harvey on purpose. And yet you, the person she should've been able to count on through all of it, you just kicked her while she was down."

"So we're not holding back punches, I see," Marsha said as she pursed her lips.

"I'm not done," Alexis voiced over Marsha.

"Your kids. They adore you. And you barely have time for them. Ever. They are so desperate for your love, they sometimes even look to me for it. The woman they've been taught to hate by you. And when you do have time for them? You take them along to things you like to do, try to make them into mini me's of the most despicable person I know."

Alexis's chest heaved as she said all that she'd ever wished to say to Marsha.

"What about you?" Marsha asked, her eyes full of accusation.

"What about me?"

"You hide behind this caring façade, but when it came down to it, you went after what you wanted. Even when it hurt my kids."

"What are you talking about?"

"They needed more time after our divorce. They were healing from the greatest trauma in their life. You just swept in, telling them your love for their dad was enough. Who was it enough for? Maybe for you but definitely not for them! So don't try to act like you were the selfless one here." Marsha held her ribs after her rant, but Alexis didn't feel badly at all.

"Seriously? We're going to start throwing around the selfish card? Because, girl, you should know. I have never met a more selfish human being on the planet. And I've met a real housewife," Alexis spat. Alexis could not believe that Marsha had just gone there.

"I'm not saying I wasn't selfish. I was. I still am. We all are. But unlike you, I can admit it."

Alexis took a step back. An uppercut wouldn't have hit harder. Was that true?

After a few moments, the initial sting of Marsha's words had worn off, and Alexis could think about them without wanting to throw something at the person who'd spoken them. As Alexis reflected, she realized Marsha was kind of right. Alexis should've waited to start dating Jared. In fact, she'd known that but had gone against her better judgement because of how much she cared for him. And that had been selfish.

"What I'm saying is, I don't have to like you, but I have to trust you. If you are going to be around my kids, I have to know that you can admit your faults. You can see when you've made a mistake. Because you're right. I am surrounded by the greatest of people. We both will be. If I let you in. Since the accident, I've had lots of time to dwell on my mistakes over the past few years. What I've learned? My biggest fault was not seeing my own faults. It's the same for you. I need you to see that or it's not fair to those we love, especially my children."

Alexis watched as Marsha swallowed. This wasn't easy for

her. And it sure wasn't easy for Alexis either. But they were doing it for those they loved. Those greatest of people.

She needed a minute to take in what Marsha had said.

"Sit down if you need to." Marsha offered the couch across from her.

Her sitting room was completely symmetrical with two identical white couches perpendicular to the big window that overlooked Elliot Drive and the ocean. Parallel to the window were two white armchairs made of matching material to the couches. A gleaming kitchen full of stainless-steel appliances and white countertops was to Alexis's left, and a dining space, which housed a gray wood table, was just beyond that. A hallway was to Alexis's right, and that was all she could see. She had to admit, she'd thought Marsha's home would be grander than this. There was a huge, gold, gaudy chandelier in the middle of the living room, which was exactly what Alexis had expected. But other than that, she had to admit it was all decorated tastefully.

"Now or later," Marsha added.

Right. She'd been offered a seat. Alexis took it. But as far from Marsha as she could. She still didn't trust the woman, even if Marsha had made a couple of good points.

"I was being selfish. I . . ." Alexis was about to list at least part of the host of reasons why she'd been selfish, but she quickly realized that didn't matter. At least not when it came to Jared and their kids. So she refrained from going on.

"No excuses?" Marsha asked, raising a skeptical eyebrow.

"None that matter," Alexis said.

Marsha nodded. "You might not be quite the lost case I assumed."

Was that approval from Marsha? Maybe not given in the kindest of forms, but Alexis would take it.

"Is my selfishness the only reason you hated me?" Alexis

asked, no longer scared of what Marsha would say. Marsha didn't like her. She probably never would. But at least Alexis could have open communication with the woman who was the mother of the kids she hoped would one day have a permanent part in her life.

"Um, no," Marsha laughed. The sound wasn't quite spiteful, but it was close. "There were so many reasons. You play the victim like no other. Your mom has been handed at least as many hard knocks as you have, but she's the one always comforting you. I may not be Margie's biggest fan, but at least she's strong. You crumpled like a paper box under a fist anytime something came your way. It's so dang annoying."

Alexis felt ire build in her chest, but she'd asked for this. She couldn't very well be upset with Marsha for her answers, could she?

"I'll admit you've gotten a little better over the last year or so, but you're still so fragile. I think that's why Jared loves you in a way he never loved me. You don't need independence the way I do," Marsha said.

Or it could be that Jared knew Alexis would be loyal, unlike cheating Marsha. But Alexis kept her thoughts to herself.

"And . . . oh, this might be the worst part of all."

Great, Alexis thought.

"You feel the need to replace me in every part of my life. First with Lou. Then with my dad. Then Jared. Finally, my kids. It's like you want to be the new me. And we all know you'll never measure up."

Ouch. Did Marsha really think that was Alexis's overall goal? Replace Marsha in every part of her life? Who would choose to do that? Not anyone who'd ever met Marsha, that was for sure.

"Do you really think that's what I want? I can't help who I fell in love with. And we all know we can't choose who our parents fall in love with. Believe me, if I could have given myself any space from you, I would have," Alexis retorted.

Marsha narrowed her eyes as she surveyed Alexis.

"And, for the record, I liked Jared first. Back when everyone still called him Ethan," Alexis added. It was definitely a petty point to make, but right now, Alexis was fine being petty.

"Ugh. I'm glad I made him go by his middle name. Can you imagine if we still called him Ethan?" Marsha asked.

Alexis was going to treat that as a rhetorical question because, personally, she missed calling him Ethan. To her, the name suited him better. But Jared was his name now, and she wasn't about to pull a Marsha on him and ask him to go by another name.

"So why am I here?" Alexis asked, sick of being put down. She'd assumed this wasn't going to be a pleasant meeting, but this was getting to be downright painful. Granted, she'd brought some of the insults on herself when she'd asked Marsha to be honest with her.

Marsha took a blanket that was draped over the couch and covered herself with it as she once again took Alexis in. Alexis had no idea what Marsha was looking for, but she was going to guess the woman would find her lacking.

"What?" Alexis asked when Marsha continued to stay silent.

"You know you really aren't as sweet as everyone thinks you are."

"What can I say? You tend to bring out the ugliest side of me."

"It isn't an attractive quality to blame your faults on someone else," Marsha spouted.

Alexis was done. She'd had her confidence knocked down a peg or two, but she'd also gotten some good answers. She'd appreciated what Marsha had said about her not seeing her own faults. It was something she should work on. There was nothing like the shame of having one of your negative characteristics pointed out by the person who hated you most to make you get a move on improving. Alexis was going to do that. Just as soon as she left this place.

She moved to stand.

"Wait," Marsha demanded.

Yeah, that wasn't going to happen. She'd given Marsha enough of her time.

"I promise I started all of this with a destination in mind," Marsha said.

Alexis was standing but didn't start walking away. She was willing to hear about two more sentences.

"I don't like you."

There was one sentence. Alexis stepped forward.

"But if I can trust you, I won't stand in the way of you and Jared," Marsha spoke too quickly.

Alexis couldn't be sure she'd heard right.

"What did you say?" Alexis asked, flopping back onto the couch behind her. She needed extra support right now.

"I don't like you—"

"Yeah, yeah, yeah. After that," Alexis said, leaning forward in her seat.

Marsha twisted her lips as if she were in pain. She probably was because she was about to give Alexis all she'd ever hoped for.

"That's why I brought up the part where you can't see your own faults. If you can work on that, I think I trust you enough to be around my kids. For now," Marsha said, not promising anything but still giving more than Alexis had ever anticipated. Was Marsha saying what Alexis thought she was saying?

"You love Jared. And the idiot loves you back. Who knows why," Marsha said.

The insults were rolling off of Alexis's back now. Nothing could get her down.

"I'll work on seeing my faults, I swear." Alexis was happy to make any and every promise.

"I believe it. You may think I was too self-absorbed to notice anything, but I saw what I needed to. You would do anything for Jared and, in turn, anything for our kids," Marsha admitted with a frown on her face. "I've already told the kids that Jared and I are done forever. I also told them that it was my choice not to live in our family home. They didn't seem too surprised. I think they were holding on to hope just because of me, and I feel like the worst mother in the world for that."

That did kind of make her the worst mother in the world, but Alexis stayed quiet. She wasn't about to say anything to upset this precarious balance of hatred and acceptance right now.

"They still aren't ready for you to come sweeping in. They need time to mourn the idea that our family really is going to look different from here on out. But . . ." Marsha paused, Alexis hanging on her every word, "If you can wait a good amount of time, at least a month—"

Alexis nodded. She could totally do that.

"I won't do anything on purpose that would hurt the relationship you have with my ex."

"Thank you, Marsha," Alexis said with tears in her eyes. Was this really happening?

"Don't thank me. I definitely won't do anything to help the two of you either."

"I wouldn't expect that."

"I should hope not," Marsha snapped.

Alexis was too joyful to let anything get her down, including Marsha's annoyed tone.

"I'm not doing this for you. I'm doing this for Jared," Marsha said quietly. "He deserved better than the way I treated him. For better or worse, he wants you. And you seem to treat him well. But I can promise if you do anything to hurt the three of them—"

Marsha's threats were left unspoken as Alexis interrupted her. "There isn't much we agree on. But we love those three with our very souls. You don't have to threaten me in order for me to treat them the best I possibly can."

Marsha eyed Alexis and then finally nodded.

Alexis stood, not knowing what else to do or say. This conversation felt over.

But ever the optimist, Alexis had to say one last thing before she left Marsha's apartment. "I know you still hate me. I get that. But know that I've never hated you. Disliked you a lot, yes. But not enough that I don't ever see a future in which we could actually act like sisters. We already have the brutally honest and fighting parts down."

Alexis smiled with her back against the front door. Marsha didn't even look up to say, "I wouldn't hold your breath."

"I won't. But if I were you, I wouldn't say never either," Alexis said as she opened the door and slipped out.

"Never!" Marsha shouted before Alexis shut the door.

Yeah, Alexis was wearing her down.

CHAPTER ELEVEN

"ARE you sure you have to go?" Nora asked Mack as he stood from where they'd been cuddling together on the couch. It was nearly ten am, time for Mack's shift at the art gallery where they both worked. Nora used to work days with Mack, but when they'd started dating, Deb, the gallery owner and Nora's sister, had put them on opposite shifts. Well, after she'd caught Nora and Mack making out in the storage area like teenagers, so Nora couldn't really blame her sister for that decision. And even though Nora missed working with Mack, she had to admit their commissions were up by a lot now that they weren't fighting for the same sales.

"Only if I want to keep my job," Mack said with a wink.

Nora grinned. "Well in that case, stay," she said. "Pretty sure with you gone, I'll get this month's sales bonus."

Mack chuckled. "That would be the only way you could win it."

Nora gasped. "Oh, it is so on," she declared.

Mack continued chuckling as he glanced at a very specific finger on Nora's left hand. "Can't let you win it this month, Love. I'm saving for something special."

Nora's stomach fluttered at the implication. Sure, she and Mack imagined they'd be together forever, so marriage was the next step. But this was . . . amazing.

"See you tonight," Mack said before giving Nora a lingering kiss and then leaving quickly.

Smart man. Nora had been about to pull him back down onto the couch with her.

Just as Mack closed the door behind him, Nora's phone began ringing.

"Hey, Mama Nora," Amber said as Nora answered a Face-time call from her daughter.

"Hey. To what do I owe this kind of call?" Nora asked.

Amber grinned on the other end of the phone. "Can't a birth daughter just want to see her beautiful birth mother's face?" Amber asked sweetly.

"Now you're making me nervous," Nora replied with a raised eyebrow.

Amber laughed. "I promise it's a good thing. I just wanted to see your face when I told you the news," she said.

Nora's eyes went wide. Amber had done it. She'd told Elise the truth about why she was getting married so quickly and all was well. "Elise isn't moving?" she asked, thrilled for Amber and Elise.

"Oh, no." Amber's eyes dropped.

Nora and her big mouth. Now she felt terrible.

"I'm so sorry—" she began.

"No, it's fine. No news from Elise yet; I'm hoping she's dropped the whole idea. So maybe you're right," Amber said brightly. "Or at least I have some time until she makes the move."

Nora smiled. She hoped that was the case as well. It wasn't like Elise to keep anything from Amber, so if she wasn't talking about the move anymore, maybe it really wasn't happening. That would be amazing news. But apparently, not the news

Amber wanted to share. Nora had learned her lesson and was now going to wait for Amber to speak.

"So I've been working with Genevieve . . ." Amber said.

Nora knew that. Many of the hours Amber spent at work were with their biggest client. Not only was Genevieve paying the girls a staggering amount of money, they knew that if Genevieve was pleased with the event, she'd spread the news near and far. Giving the girls and their lodge the kind of publicity money couldn't buy.

"How has that been?" Nora asked.

"She's nice," Amber said, her voice a little high pitched for her to be telling the whole truth.

"And . . . ?" Nora asked.

"I think after meeting Julia, I assumed I'd pegged all Hollywood actresses wrong. Julia is the opposite of a diva. But Genevieve lives up to every letter of the word. She likes things her way and now. There is no alternative."

Nora chuckled because Amber didn't seem to be feeling down because of her difficult client. It was more like Genevieve was just a puzzle she needed to figure out.

"But it's been great. She's keeping me busy and, so far, hasn't asked the impossible."

"Good," Nora said, wondering if that was the news. She hoped she'd given enough of a facial reaction to make the video call worth it.

"But Genevieve did ask for something new at our last meeting," Amber said.

Nora nodded.

"Twelve watercolor depictions of their favorite engagement photos."

Nora specialized in watercolor. Maybe that was why Amber was telling her this? To get her opinion about whether the artist Genevieve had chosen was a good one?

"That sounds like quite the task, but I'm sure many artists would be up for it. What exactly is she looking for?" Nora asked.

"You," Amber said.

Nora's mouth dropped open. Was this a joke? It had to be. Kids were always pulling pranks for social media these days. Maybe this was a new promo for their business? Elise and Amber pranking those they loved?

Nora closed her mouth. If she was being recorded, she didn't want to look ridiculous.

"Seriously, Amber," Nora chided, letting her know the joke was over.

"I *am* being serious. She started talking about her vision by explaining that when she was at her dear friend Julia's home a couple of weeks ago, she saw a beautiful piece of art. A watercolor portrait of Julia," Amber explained.

Oh. Nora had almost forgotten she'd given that to Julia for her birthday two months before.

A couple of weeks before Julia's birthday, Julia, Nora, and Deb had decided to get together for lunch one afternoon at Bess's food truck. They'd gotten their food and eaten at one of the picnic tables that overlooked the ocean. During their conversation, Julia had laughed really hard. Nora couldn't remember what they'd been talking about, but she'd been struck by how at ease Julia appeared—a stark contrast to the Julia who'd arrived on their island. The moment had stuck in Nora's mind, so she'd gone home and painted it. Nora had learned early on that the only way to get those moments to stop nagging her was to get them on canvas. But it made no sense for Nora to keep the portrait, so she'd given it to Julia for her birthday. Julia had said she loved it, but Nora had wondered if it was a weird gift to give.

"She said it was the perfect mix of whimsical and realistic," Amber said, interrupting Nora's thoughts. Right, Genevieve wanted her to paint . . . what was it? Twelve portraits?

"When Julia explained that you were a local artist as well as her friend, Genevieve knew she had to commission some art by you. So she told me to track you down. When I said that that might be easier than anticipated since you're my birth mom, she cackled with glee."

Amber's eyes were bright with excitement. "I've never seen anything like it, but she should be cast as a witch next because she sure has the laugh down."

Nora wanted to respond, but she was still in shock.

"She was like, 'Isn't this serendipitous?' And then she reminded herself that she'd been the one to insist we host her wedding. So really it was her that had put together the perfect circumstances, making her a genius. She then proceeded to get every person in the room with her and on the other side of the video call with me to call her a genius. She made Dan, her fiancé, admit it twice."

Amber giggled but then stopped. "You haven't said a word. Are you okay?"

Nora realized her daughter was right. But what was she supposed to say? This was the kind of honor she'd only ever dreamed of. A patron seeing her art and demanding to commission her? She'd literally sat up at night imagining this moment would happen. And now it was happening. With Genevieve Porter, no less.

"I'm fine. Great. Stupendous. This is a lot," Nora said, feeling silly about the words coming out of her mouth. But she couldn't help it.

Amber giggled. "Stupendous. Perfect word choice. So I take it you're interested in the job?"

Nora thought about the types of guests Genevieve would surely have at her wedding. They would all be seeing her art. Nora's breathing sped up. They would be seeing her art. What if she couldn't get them all done in time? What if they weren't good? What if Genevieve hated them?

"Get out of your head, Mama Nora," Amber demanded.

Nora looked at her phone to see the panicked expression on her face. No wonder Amber could read her thoughts.

"I don't know if I can do it," Nora admitted.

Amber's eyes narrowed in determination. "She loved your work. She wants you. You can draw a few sketches of what you plan on doing for her pictures and see if she likes it. If she doesn't, no skin off your back. But if she does, imagine this opportunity for you. I know you like working for Aunt Deb and you love your tiny little apartment. I also know that you have most of your nest egg invested in this lodge right now. So even if you wanted a bigger place or wanted to stop working for a bit, you wouldn't be able to. The Lodge is doing better than we expected, but it will still be a while until you see a complete return on your investment. However, with what Genevieve is willing to pay you, you could get your own art studio right now. You could stop working for a few months to travel. Or you could even put a down payment on that house you think I don't know you've been eyeing."

Amber then told Nora what Genevieve would pay for the portraits, and Nora promptly dropped her phone.

Amber's laugh sounded from the floor where Nora's phone now lay.

"Did you tell her that's too much?" Nora replied as she worked on picking up her phone with shaky hands.

"No I didn't. It's a perfectly respectable amount for a sought-after artist doing twelve paintings in the next six months," Amber said.

"Sought-after?" Nora asked skeptically.

"Yes," Amber said with no hesitation. "So can I tell her you accept? You'll make my life truly difficult if you don't."

Amber knew that was the nail in the coffin. There was no way Nora would deny her this. And it really was the opportunity of a lifetime. Was she going to squander it because she was afraid? No.

"You can," Nora said, feeling like she might faint. She breathed deeply as she laid down on her couch. She just needed a minute to catch her breath.

"Awesome," Amber replied. It looked like she was about to say more but knocking sounded on her office door.

"Come in," Amber called.

"Oh, are you on with Genevieve?" Nora heard Elise whisper.

"Nope. It's Mama Nora."

"Oh hey, Mama Nora," Elise said brightly as her face filled the frame next to her sister.

"Hey, Elise. You look excited," Nora said. She was still lying down on the couch, but at least she could now breathe.

"I am. But first, did you hear your news?" Elise asked.

"I did," Nora said.

"That's why she's incapacitated on her couch right now," Amber teased.

The women all laughed.

"So it's time for my news?" Elise asked before looking warily at her sister. But then her huge smile returned.

Uh oh. Nora was pretty sure she knew what Elise was about to say.

"Sure," Amber said. She'd been looking at something on her desk, so she'd missed the glance Elise had given her.

"I found an apartment," Elise said.

Nora's stomach dropped at the same time all color drained from Amber's face.

"Oh," Amber said.

Nora felt like she shouldn't be listening in on this conversation, but at the same time, she wanted to be there for the girls.

"Exciting, right?" Elise asked.

"Yeah, super," Amber said, attempting cheer.

"I know this is sudden, and I'll miss you so much. But it's also an adventure," Elise said.

Amber nodded slowly.

"So let's make this fun," Elise said, her voice too bright.

"Yeah, for sure," Amber replied.

"I was thinking we could have a packing party tonight after work?" Elise asked.

"So soon?" Amber asked, her voice hitching on the word *soon*.

"I found this can't miss apartment, and they'll have it open for me in three days. I still have a bit more training for Carol so that she'll be ready to take over for me here, but I think I can get that done as well as pack all my stuff as long as you're able to help."

Amber nodded, her face still a little too pale. "Yeah, of course."

"Mama Nora, I'd love for you to come too," Elise said into the phone with a gigantic smile on her face.

Nora glanced from the fake smile on Elise's face to the fake one on Amber's. "I wouldn't miss it."

NORA GOT to Amber and Elise's cute little cottage a few hours later and was about to knock on the screen door when she heard that she was interrupting a conversation. She couldn't see in because the waning sunlight made it too hard to view anything on the other side of the door.

"So you were serious about this?" Amber asked.

"I told you I was moving, Amber."

"After I told you I was getting married. I thought it was a gut reaction and you'd rethink it and decide that you couldn't leave me right now."

"Amber," Elise's sigh was loud enough for Nora to hear outside. "I have to do this."

"Why? Why now?" Amber asked.

"Because we need someone in Seattle, and it makes sense for me to be that someone."

"Carol could do it. I know we were looking out of house for someone to fill that position, but Carol would be perfect for the job."

"I'm training Carol to take over for me here," Elise said.

"So why not switch it?"

Nora wasn't sure if she should back away or not. She was supposed to be here but not eavesdropping. And yet she couldn't bring herself to back away, so instead she waited silently behind the door.

"Because I can't be here right now. I think we need some space from each other," Elise said.

"The way you've been ignoring me for the last two weeks hasn't been enough space?" Amber asked, hurt filling her voice.

"That's not fair," Elise replied.

"It's the truth," Amber said. "If it doesn't have to do with work, we don't talk about it."

"I asked if you wanted me to make you dinner last night or if you were going out with Raul."

"Why do you say his name like that?" Amber asked.

"Like what?"

"Raul," Amber said, emphasizing the last syllable.

"Isn't that how you say his name?"

"Yes, but no. You used to say Mr. Checker's name like that in high school, remember?" Amber asked.

Nora had no idea what answer Elise gave because it was a silent one.

"And you hated him."

"This is silly, Amber. I don't hate Raul. I don't know him."

"So your solution to that is to leave? How can you get to know him then? It doesn't make sense."

"No, you want to know what doesn't make sense? You marrying a man you just barely met. This isn't like you, Amber. And now I'm saying the things I promised to keep to myself. Things that will hurt you but that I'm bound to say if I stay. Because right now, I can't be happy for you. And I hate that." Elise's voice sounded strained, and Nora knew the tears had begun.

"I need you to be happy for me, Elise. Don't you get it? None of this can happen without you. I need you," Amber said, and it was easy to hear her tears as well.

Nora's stomach knotted, part of her telling her to leave right now while the other part said it would be best to stay. These girls were going to need her soon.

"I don't know what to say. I won't lie to you," Elise replied.

"I know it's out of character for me to be getting married this fast. But I love him. Can't you trust that I'm making the right decision?"

"But why? It just makes no sense. You always talked about dating a guy for at least a year before you got engaged and then another year before you got married. It's been barely that many months," Elise said.

"He's going to have to leave the US," Amber said, and then Nora heard the sound of a hand slapping against skin. Nora was going to venture a guess that Amber was slapping a hand over her mouth.

"He's what?" Elise asked.

"I love him. I can't let him leave," Amber said, but even Nora knew it was too late. If Amber had presented the situation better, maybe Elise would've been on her side. But this was maybe the most terrible way Amber could have told Elise.

"He asked you to marry him knowing he'd have to return home if he didn't find another way to stay in the United States?" Elise asked.

"It isn't like that. I asked him to marry me so that he could stay."

"You're marrying him so that he can stay?"

"No, I'm marrying him because I can't stand the idea of him leaving." Amber begged Elise to understand.

"How is he working for us? I don't get it. I thought work visas are good for like seven years?"

"He's still using his visa from his last job. That's why he leaves the island so often. He goes back to work for them a couple of times a week so that he can keep his old visa. He could always go home and we could begin the process of getting him a new work visa under us, but why do that when we can just get married?"

Nora cringed. Amber was so nervous that she was botching this big time.

"So you're marrying him so we don't have to bother with getting him a new work visa?"

"Elise, stop being purposefully obtuse. I love him. I would be marrying him anyway!"

"Yes, but when?"

Silence sounded for a minute, and Nora knew it was either knock now or leave now. She opted for the former. She couldn't leave her girls like this. She put her hand up to knock when her movement was interrupted by Elise speaking.

"You can come in, Mama Nora," Elise said.

Nora opened the door to see Elise facing her. Nora quickly realized that Elise had been able to see her waiting outside the whole time from her position at the kitchen table facing the door. Nora had just assumed that because the screen made things too dark for her to see them, they also couldn't see her. She was mistaken. Although, Amber hadn't been able to see her since her seat at the table was with her back to the door.

"You heard all of that, right?" Elise asked.

Nora nodded shamefully.

"Good. Then we don't have to catch you up to speed," Amber said.

Oh, thank goodness they weren't upset with her.

"I noticed your lack of reaction about the visa expiring thing. You knew?" Elise asked, the puckering around her mouth and eyes showing hurt.

"Amber talked to me about it a few nights ago," Nora said nervously. She didn't want to add any more fuel to the girls' fight.

"And you're okay with it?" Elise asked, now her tone laced with hurt as well.

Nora had no idea how to answer that question. Either possibility seemed like a betrayal to one of the girls. She couldn't do that to them.

"I believe that Amber truly loves Raul," Nora said, hoping to stay neutral but also say what she felt.

No one gasped at Nora's words, so she figured she'd done what she'd set out to do. The only reaction was a slight nod from Elise before she turned back to Amber. "Are you going to answer my question?"

Nora was wracking her mind for a question. Oh right. When would Amber have decided to marry Raul if it weren't for the threat of him needing to leave the country.

"I don't know. I can't say because the situation is what it is. I can't change that."

"You can't say or won't say?" Elise asked. When Amber didn't respond, Elise went on. "Do Mom and Dad know?"

Amber shook her head.

"We have to tell them."

"*I* have to tell them," Amber amended.

"Now."

"I'm not ready."

"So you can tell Mama Nora but not Mom and Dad?"

"You know how they get, Elise. They won't understand. Not with the situation the way it is. I need them to like Raul before telling them."

Elise gasped, understanding marking her features.

"You weren't planning on telling any of us, were you?" Elise asked, her eyes wide. "If it weren't for this mistaken outburst, you would have never told me."

"I would've," Amber denied too softly.

"After the wedding?" Elise countered.

Amber didn't answer giving Elise all she needed to know.

Elise stood from the table and began pacing the small living space in their cottage. These girls had shared everything. A home, a room, a bathroom, a job, and even a dream. Nora could see how Amber keeping anything from Elise would throw the balance of their relationship off kilter. Maybe Elise was right in leaving. Maybe the girls were too reliant on one another.

"This isn't you, Amber. And if it isn't you, it has to be him."

"That's not it," Amber argued with tears in her eyes.

Elise stopped her pacing and looked at her sister. "Then call Mom and Dad. Give us the chance to weigh in and give you advice when we're armed with all the facts. It's only fair," Elise demanded.

Amber dropped her head as Nora stood awkwardly at the corner of the table between her and Elise. What was she supposed to do? She had to help. But what could she do or say to make any of this okay?

"Fine," Amber said, looking up at Elise and pulling her phone from her pocket. "I have nothing to be ashamed of."

"It's not *your* misbehavior I'm worried about," Elise muttered as Amber dialed her mom.

"Hey, Mom," Amber said after Tabby answered her call.

"I'm here too, Mom," Elise said since Amber had put the call on speaker.

"As well as Nora," Amber added.

"Good to hear from you all," Tabby gushed. Little did she know what was in store for her.

"Is Dad around?" Amber asked.

"Yeah. Let me just go to his office," Tabby said. "I take it you have some news? Wedding related?" Tabby asked as she walked.

"You could say that," Amber said.

Elise pursed her lips.

"Okay, I have your dad on as well," Tabby spoke.

"Hey, girls," Gerry said.

"And Nora," Tabby added.

"Oh, and Nora." The smile Gerry wore was heard in his tone.

"They have wedding news," Tabby said to Gerry.

"Wonderful," Gerry said.

But even Nora, who didn't know Gerry that well, could hear that he was trying too hard. That the idea of wedding news wasn't as wonderful as he was trying to make it appear.

"It's not exactly wedding news," Amber said.

"Or good news," Elise muttered.

Amber glared at her sister.

"It's just some information about Raul," Amber said.

"And it isn't good news?" Tabby asked nervously.

"No. I mean *no* it isn't bad news," Amber replied, still glaring at Elise.

"What?" Elise asked. "I'm just telling the truth. Something you haven't done these past few weeks."

"I wasn't lying," Amber countered.

"It was a lie of omission," Elise stated.

"What's going on?" Gerry asked.

"I want to preface this with *I love Raul*. I would be marrying him no matter the circumstances."

"You just wouldn't be marrying him now," Elise interrupted.

Amber's eyes went wide with frustration. "Will you quit it?!"

"Will you tell the whole truth?" Elise asked. "I know you wouldn't have revealed that little tidbit had I not asked the exact right question. Mom and Dad should know all the facts."

"You wouldn't be marrying Raul?" Tabby asked, her confusion apparent.

"I would be," Amber answered.

"But not now," Elise added.

"Out!" Amber screamed in a voice Nora had never heard. Amber pointed to their front door. "This isn't a game. This isn't the time to have to get the last word. This is my life!"

Amber's chest heaved.

Elise shook her head. "Do you think I'm doing this to hurt you? Everything I'm doing and saying is because I understand how very vital all of this is and I need to protect you. I love you more than anyone else in the world. But if you think I'm treating this like some joke because I think it's fun to make you sad, then you don't know me at all." Elise stood and left the cottage the way Amber had commanded, slamming the screen door behind her.

Tears streamed down Amber's face. "This is supposed to be such a blissful time."

Nora blinked back her own tears.

"Amber?" Gerry asked.

"Elise left," Amber said.

"We gathered that. Are you okay, Sweetheart?" Tabby asked.

"No," Amber replied.

She swallowed, trying to rein in her emotions.

"What did you need to tell us?" Gerry asked, seeming to know that that would get to the root of the issue.

"I would be marrying Raul regardless," Amber said.

"We get that, Honey," Tabby said.

"He's going to have to leave the US. At the beginning of next year. When I realized I'd fallen in love with him and knew he was the one for me, I was the one who suggested we get married so that he could stay. I was the one who didn't want to be apart from him. He can come back on his own. He doesn't need me. His only reason to stay is for me. Because I want him to," Amber stated.

"Who asked who out first, Amber?" Gerry asked.

"He asked me. But that doesn't mean—"

"He knew he'd have to return home soon then, didn't he?" Gerry asked.

"Yes, but does that mean he shouldn't have dated at all?" Amber pleaded for her parents to understand.

"I think what your father is trying to say is that even though it feels like you initiated every part of getting married and Raul staying, that may not be the case," Tabby said slowly, as if she were trying to comprehend her own words as she spoke them.

"What I'm saying is this feels like all the more reason for you both to enter into this union at a slower pace," Gerry added.

Amber shook her head. "I know I love him and I want to be with him forever. Why would I slow things down just so that he can leave?"

"Why don't you want him to leave?" Gerry asked.

"Because I'll miss him so much, I won't be able to survive it," Amber said softly.

"Oh, Sweetheart. I know it feels like that. But you will be able to survive it."

"What if I don't want to? I don't want that hurt. And I can avoid it. So why wouldn't I?"

"So that you can know you are doing the right thing. When the blooms of this immediate and urgent love fade, what will be left?" Tabby asked.

"The new love we'll grow because we'll be together," Amber declared.

"And you know that you'll be this sure about Raul in five, ten years?" Gerry asked.

"I can't know that," Amber retorted.

"But you can be surer," Gerry replied.

"You really think that? That if I wait the two years I always imagined, I'll be sure and our marriage will be that much more rock solid?" Amber asked, sounding exasperated.

"Marriage needs a foundation. What do you have as your foundation?" Tabby asked.

"Love," Amber replied.

"And?" Gerry asked.

"And admiration. And I've never been more satisfied with life than with Raul by my side."

"And?" Tabby asked.

"There needs to be more?" Amber asked.

"Please wait to get married," Tabby pleaded.

"We didn't want to say anything before, but we're nervous for you Amber. And with this new news, we can't help but voice our concerns."

"So are you forbidding me from getting married? Like some medieval movie where parents sold their daughters into marriage?"

"You know that's not the case, Amber." Tabby sounded hurt.

"We know that you are a grown woman. You are smart and capable. What we are *asking* is for you to take a step or two back. Take some time," Gerry said.

"Let Raul leave," Amber uttered.

"If necessary, yes," Gerry said, sounding as patient as ever.

"How will I know if it's necessary? Excuse me, how will *we* know if it's necessary? Because, evidently, who I marry and how I marry him is now a group decision," Amber replied crossly.

"We want you to be happy," Tabby said instead of answering Amber's question.

Amber sagged against the back of her chair, as if her mom's kind words had knocked the fight right out of her.

"It doesn't feel like it right now," Amber said softly.

"I know, Sweetheart. And I hate that."

"I hate it too," Amber said, her tears starting up again now that her anger had waned.

"Keep dating Raul. You have six months until he has to leave. Give yourself those full six months. You could always marry him in Argentina. Wouldn't that be romantic?" Tabby asked.

Amber blinked back tears. "But then he'd already be gone. Bringing him back to the US will take time."

"You could have a prolonged honeymoon in South America," Tabby said.

"So what you're saying is, if I keep with my present plan, none of you can celebrate with me?" Amber said.

"None of us said that," Tabby said quickly.

"But it was implied. You all want me to wait. And then after some time, get married."

"If that's what you still want," Gerry said.

"Gerry," Tabby muttered.

"Of course we assume you'll still want to marry Raul. We

don't want you two to break up. We just want you two to know one another better," Tabby said.

Amber nodded stoically. "I get it," she said.

"Do you?" Tabby asked hopefully.

"I knew you would. You've always had a good head on your shoulders," Gerry added.

"Yeah, I do," Amber said, turning the phone in her hands.

"Well, I guess we should let you go and make up with your sister," Tabby said eagerly. It was apparent she felt they'd dodged a bullet.

"Yeah," Amber deadpanned, but her parents didn't seem to notice her lack of enthusiasm.

Nora couldn't miss it. Maybe because she could see the frown that stretched down to Amber's chin.

"Good night, Amber," Gerry said.

"We love you," Tabby added.

"Love you too," Amber said before hanging up and setting the phone on the table.

"They aren't ever going to get it, are they?" she asked Nora.

"They want what's best for you," Nora said, aching to comfort Amber.

"They want what they think is best for me," Amber amended.

Maybe that was true. But Nora could see both sides of the situation too well to bind herself to a stance.

"I think I need to take a walk," Amber said as she stood.

"Oh, okay," Nora said, realizing Amber needed some time alone. "But it's getting dark—"

"I'll be careful," Amber promised. Then she looked at Nora. "Thank you."

Nora wasn't sure what Amber was grateful for, but with the genuine way she'd said the words, Nora was glad she'd done whatever she'd done.

"You're welcome," Nora said as they both walked toward the door.

They left the cottage, Nora walking to her car as Amber walked in the opposite direction of the lodge toward the sea cliffs.

Unlike Amber's parents, Nora felt no peace as she had to drive away. She was sure they were nowhere near the end of this journey and that Amber might be about to make a whole lot of decisions none of them would approve of.

CHAPTER TWELVE

LOU TRIED to keep the look of disgust off her face as she walked through the gym. It was eight am, for goodness' sake. How was this place packed? Didn't these people have kids to get to school? Jobs to go to? How were they all able to spend hours on end here? And for what? To better live up to society's standard of beauty? It really was a shame.

And she was adding to this culture by providing the gym. Granted, her dad owned the place, but Lou ran it. Without her, the gym would close, and maybe people would spend more time with their families or doing something equally important.

Lou tried to ignore the little voice that told her a person being here was a good thing. Not only were they working on their physical strength, often someone who took the time to work out consistently was mentally in a better place as well. Lou ignored the memories of the days she used to work out on a nearly daily basis and how good she'd felt about herself. Not because she'd been any more beautiful but because she'd felt strong. In some ways, almost invincible. Now she crumbled to the ground when her ex visited, hiding evidence of the binging she now did more often than she ever had while working out consistently.

"I can't believe you're here, Lou. With that kind of news, I wouldn't have been able to show my face in public for weeks. Maybe months. But look at you. Here at work. At a gym. Even though it's obvious you never actually use the facility. You are brave in so many ways."

Lou looked over to see that the person speaking to her was none other than Jamie. The same woman who'd first given her the news that Harvey was, indeed, dating Felicity. When he'd supposedly been trying to repair what he had with Lou.

Lou tried to smile at Jamie and her backhanded compliments. Because even though Lou knew Jamie wasn't being at all serious when she called her brave, Lou was going to put on the facade she had to to get through this conversation. And then, if she needed to go into her office to break down, she would.

She could feel the excitement exuding from Jamie because of the bad news she was about to share. Lou wasn't sure what she'd ever done to Jamie for the woman to take such pleasure in her pain. Jamie and Felicity were at least five years younger than Lou, so it wasn't an unresolved issue from their school days. Honestly, both women seemed to have some sort of vendetta against her, and Lou hadn't even really known who either was until Felicity had begun dating Harvey. But what she did know was that this woman wanted her to grovel for information. And she wasn't about to do that. So she did the exact opposite.

"That's kind of you to say," Lou said, pretending she hadn't understood that what Jamie had said wasn't kind at all. Then she continued her walk toward her office.

She could imagine Jamie's slack-jawed expression behind her and smiled a bit. She was still afraid of whatever news Jamie had, but that had been fun.

"So you don't care that Harvey asked Felicity to move in

with him last night?" Jamie called out loudly enough for nearly every person in their vicinity to hear.

Redness filled Lou's cheeks, embarrassment and frustration that she still cared about what Harvey was doing with another woman overcoming her. Even after all he'd put her through, this still hurt. And the fact that a crowded room in the gym was witness to this scene helped nothing.

"Why should I?" Lou was able to manage as she tried to keep walking, but her knees felt unable to carry their load.

"Because that's one step closer to marriage. I'm sure you'll be thrilled for those sweet kiddos of yours to have a brand-new stepmom."

Joke was on Jamie. Harvey didn't spend enough time with his kids for Felicity to have any impact on her kids. But she could. If Harvey did end up marrying this woman who had such obvious disdain for Lou and then they decided to have her kids in their life. How could Lou stop them? She couldn't.

Her wobbly knees now joined leaden feet, and Lou worried she was moments away from tipping over. She would have sat on the weight bench next to her if she didn't need to get out of there. Now.

"Hey, Lou."

Lou was grateful that any voice other than Jamie's was saying her name.

"What's up?" Lou asked brightly, looking to see that it was Deb who'd called out to her. Lou didn't know Deb well, but Bess, Alexis's boss, was Deb's best friend. So of course Lou had interacted with her a bit. Still, she was kind of surprised that an acquaintance was interrupting her conversation.

"Do you mind announcing over the sound system that a red Charger is about to be towed? The license plate is—" Deb said when Jamie yelped.

"That's my car!" she shouted, scurrying out of the gym at a speed Lou didn't know the woman was capable of moving at.

Deb quickly moved to Lou's side. "Let's get you to your office. I'm sure you've got a ton of work to do," she said loudly enough for those around to hear.

She was giving Lou an out so that it wouldn't look like she was rushing away to hide the minute Jamie left.

"Yeah, so much work," Lou said, her part in the charade falling short. It sounded like she was lying. Even though she wasn't. There was always a ton to do at the gym.

Lou walked the rest of the way to her office, momentarily overcoming wobbly knees and leaden feet, and she let Deb in before closing the door and sinking down onto her desk chair.

She glanced up and saw Deb watching her.

"It's fine. I mean, I'm fine. It really wasn't a big deal," Lou said.

Deb raised an eyebrow. "Are you lying to me or to yourself?" she asked.

"Both," Lou responded automatically before sighing. "Thanks for that," she quickly added when she realized she would probably still be out there if it hadn't been for Deb.

"Today was the right day for you to decide to work out at the gym instead of running outside." Lou smiled at Deb. She knew the woman typically didn't like working out inside but made exceptions, usually when the weather was bad. And today was already ridiculously hot, even though it was a quarter past eight am.

So many circumstances had come together just right for Deb to have been there when Lou needed an escape. "And what a blessing that her car was being towed."

"Um, about that," Deb said with a smirk.

"You lied?" Lou asked, equal parts shocked and impressed.

"Do you mind if I hide out in here until she leaves?" Deb asked as she turned toward the window in Lou's office. Lou had recently upgraded her windows so that when anyone looked in, they saw a mirror. But on Lou's side it was clear so that she could watch what was going on in the gym without being obvious about it.

Lou and Deb watched as Jamie walked back into the gym, her head swiveling back and forth.

"Oh, she's pissed," Lou said grinning. She knew she shouldn't take such pleasure in this. If it were her children doing the same thing, she'd say to turn the other cheek instead of seeking retribution. But Lou wasn't feeling very charitable right about now and she was okay with laughing a little at Jamie's frustration. "You can totally stay in here as long as you need. Are you worried about the next time you see her?"

Deb laughed. "I've been introduced to Jamie three times. Each time she's glazed over me as if I don't exist. Then once she came up to me at the diner acting all nice and I thought, wow, this woman has done a one-eighty. Until she asked how often my sister got to hang out with Julia, and I realized not only was she trying to use me, she thought I was Gen. So I doubt she'll remember me."

Lou joined Deb in laughing. It felt good to let go of the tension she'd felt minutes before until she remembered what Jamie had said.

"What if Harvey marries her?" Lou asked. This was a fear she wouldn't typically speak aloud, but something about Deb not being too close but having proved herself trustworthy had Lou spilling her guts. "I don't know Felicity well. But from what I've seen, she's a lot like Jamie."

Deb watched Lou, her face full of sympathy.

"I can't have my kids spending time with a woman like that," Lou stated.

"Maybe you should sic Marsha on them," Deb said.

Lou smiled as she imagined that. Even after the accident, Marsha could easily make Jamie and Felicity cry. But she didn't want to ask her sister to go back to her callous behavior so soon after she'd turned a new leaf. And honestly, she didn't want to hurt Jamie or Felicity. It was the last thing she should be doing if she really thought Felicity could become her kids' stepmom.

Deb continued to watch Lou, and Lou wondered what she saw. A broken woman? A woman who didn't even have the strength to carry herself? A woman who had lost who she was?

Because those would all be correct observations. But Lou had no idea how to change any of it. She was stuck. In this deep rut. And no matter how hard she tried to claw her way out, she fell right back in with just some mud on her face to show for her effort.

"Harvey has made his decision. And he'll keep making decisions. No matter how much that sucks, you can do nothing about it," Deb said.

Lou frowned. Was this supposed to be making her feel better?

"You hate me right now, don't you?" Deb asked.

"I don't hate you," Lou said carefully.

"I would if I were you. Because I was in this exact place a couple of years back, and if anyone had tried to tell me what I'm telling you right now, I would've told them to go to hell."

Lou's frown became a little less severe. She remembered when Deb had gone through her divorce. From what Lou had heard, it had been messy. And Deb had kids as well, even though they were quite a bit older than Lou's kids.

"My ex had been cheating on me for years. Had a whole set up with his mistress in Europe. The pilot with a mistress in another country. Could he have been any more cliché? Granted, his mistress was American. But they flew together, so they made home base elsewhere. Anyway, I digress. None of that matters.

What did matter was that I hated him. So much. The hate I felt not only ate away at me but some days it fueled me. So I had a real love-hate relationship with my hate."

As insane as that sounded, Lou completely understood what Deb was saying. It was the exact same way she felt about her hate for Harvey. Although she still didn't purely hate him. She wanted to, but how was she supposed to completely hate the man who'd given her her beautiful children?

"And then I found Luke. The man of my dreams. He reminded me what a true partner should be like and loved me when I thought everyone should despise me. On top of that? He was the best stepdad I could've ever imagined. And I felt like things would go smoothly from there on out."

Lou nodded. She assumed if she ever found a man like Luke, her problems would feel a whole lot smaller.

"But they didn't."

Lou dropped her head against the chair behind her. Really? This was the worst pep talk of all time.

"Rich was still in my life. Forever. And I found my hate for him somehow growing. Every time he'd brush off a big event. Or wouldn't follow through on something he'd promised the kids. Or was too busy to call on their birthdays."

Lou closed her eyes. She understood forgotten birthdays. She'd cradled more than one kid on their special day when their dad just couldn't be bothered to remember his own offspring.

"I already understood that I couldn't control Rich. But I still hated him every time he messed up. And it took me a while to realize how counterintuitive that was. I was saying there was nothing I could do to make him a better dad, yet I spent so much of my time and energy trying to do just that."

"But you can't just give up on them, can you? You have to keep trying. For the sake of your kids," Lou said.

"Keep trying what?" Deb asked. "Nagging, calling them just to have your calls ignored, yelling, threatening?"

Lou had tried each of those tactics.

"Does it ever work?" Deb asked.

Lou shook her head.

"You've done absolutely everything you can when it comes to your ex, and it does nothing, right?" Deb asked.

Lou nodded. Deb was right. It was so hard to admit because that meant a lifetime of heartache for her children, unless by some grace of God, Harvey changed on his own. But Lou could do nothing more.

"And your kids deserve so much better."

Lou's eyes stung. She'd cried over this same predicament many times. Because she'd watched as her precious kids had hurt. She'd been the one who had chosen Harvey. She should be punished. Not her innocent children.

"So give it to them," Deb said.

Lou tilted her head in confusion. Hadn't Deb just said . . .

"Those hours, days, weeks, even months of worrying and contemplating how to get Harvey to change? Spend that time on you. On your relationship with your children. Your relationship with you. Spend that time bettering yourself so that your kids aren't getting just half of what their mom could be and none of their dad."

Lou's throat felt too tight. Was that what she'd been doing? Spending all her time and energy on getting Harvey to be a better man while sliding backwards as a mother and woman? She thought about her binge sessions. Her lack of motivation in all parts of life. Things that used to thrill her were now mundane. When was the last time she'd been truly full of joy? Maybe when Marsha had apologized, but that had been Marsha, not Lou. When was the last time she'd done anything for her kids besides the bare minimum and trying to bring Harvey back to them?

She couldn't even remember.

"I've heard so many women in our position say creating a better life now is the best revenge. But it isn't about that. It isn't about Harvey at all. It's about you and your children. Harvey won't be there for a school play? You're there. With a smile on your face. Enjoying yourself. Ready for the standing ovation. It won't replace that their father isn't there, but it will strengthen their relationship with their mother. They will know that you care. What more can you give your kids?"

"I've been letting them catch the bus home some days, even on my days off. Because I've been too busy wallowing," Lou admitted shamefully.

"No more wallowing if you accept that Harvey will do what Harvey wants. But your life doesn't hinge on Harvey's decisions. There will still be so many hard days. Your kids won't stop crying when Harvey disappoints them, but they will understand that even if they can't rely on one parent, they can totally and completely rely on the other. It will be enough."

Deb's words felt like a promise. A lifeline when Lou had felt all was lost.

Lou drew in a deep breath, trying to figure out where to start. No more binging. She was hurting not only herself but her kids with each binge because her loathing wasn't just for Harvey. It had stretched to herself. She hated the life she'd created for her kids. But it was what they had. What good was hating it? She could change it if she wanted to, but she would no longer hate it. Life without Harvey was a different future than she'd imagined, but that didn't mean it couldn't be beautiful.

"Looks like Jamie is on her way out," Deb said, her eyes on Lou's office window.

"I don't know how I can thank you enough. Not just for

what you did out there but in here," Lou said. She was filled with so many emotions, she didn't know how to pinpoint what she was feeling.

"Just a *thank you* is enough," Deb said with a grin. "And I should return the gratitude. Knowing that my years of pain and suffering could not only help me but now can help you? Makes it feel a lot more worth it."

Lou didn't think that was a fair trade, but she would take it.

"Oh, you can also thank me by making those changes. I know you're already thinking about some. You'll come across so many more. Most of them will be hard, things you don't want to tackle. It's easier to stay in the rut of loathing our exes. But don't stay there. It's lonely and, ultimately, it will never hurt those men who are hurting us."

Lou knew that was the truth. Harvey didn't truly care about anyone other than himself. Hopefully that would change for their kids one day, but she now knew it would never change when it came to her. He didn't have the capacity to love someone with Lou's flaws. And that was okay. Because Lou had the capacity to love someone with her flaws.

"I think I'm going to start working out again. I used to find so much joy in that," Lou said. She hadn't worked out in months. Probably since she'd given the class she'd taught to Alexis full-time. Maybe she should go back to teaching a few days a week.

"If you ever want a running partner, give me a call," Deb said.

Lou doubted that would be needed. She was more of a dancer when it came to cardio. But then again, it could happen. Lou wasn't ruling anything out.

"Will do," Lou said.

"But don't be holding my breath for that call?" Deb asked.

Lou laughed. "Something like that."

"I'll be checking up on you, Lou," Deb said as she exited the office and headed out of the gym.

Lou hoped she would. She thought about all the other things she could do now that she would no longer be thinking about how to make Harvey step up. Maybe she could coach one of the boys' soccer teams? Or she could learn how to play the guitar? Emma had been interested in that. Lessons together would be fun.

When Lou thought about Harvey, the hate and anger were still there. She hoped to one day get rid of that, but letting go of trying to control him made those emotions feel a bit more distant. And Lou could breathe again.

CHAPTER THIRTEEN

"DINNER IS SERVED," Julia said as she pulled a sheet pan out of the oven. She had finally mastered her roast chicken recipe. Sure, she and Ellis now had to eat the meal a few times a week because she didn't want to forget how to make it, but she tried to change things up a little each time. She used different nuts in the crust and now had a collection of about ten different mustards.

"Smells amazing," Wendy said as she, Ellis, and Julia gathered around the table in Julia's kitchen. For more formal events, Julia hosted in the dining room. But this was just a small family gathering. Hopefully the first of many.

Wendy had now been on the island for a few weeks. In that short time, she'd not only bought a car but she'd moved into her own apartment and had started her job at Whisling Savings. Julia wasn't sure a prouder aunt existed.

"It does. Smells even better than the last four times we had it this week," Ellis teased.

Julia swatted at him with the hot pad in her hand.

"You said you love this chicken," she pouted.

"I do. And I love the woman who makes it even more," Ellis said as he pulled Julia onto his lap and pressed his lips to hers.

"Children in the room," Wendy reminded.

"Can you still be called a child when it's legal for you to drink?" Ellis asked as Julia jumped off his lap.

"Are you ready to take me out to a bar?" Wendy asked.

"No." Ellis's eyes went wide at just the idea.

"And I'm not ready to see you make out with my aunt," Wendy replied.

"Touché," Ellis said as Julia laughed.

She was finding there was no greater feeling in the world than having family close. Who would've thought? Julia, the woman who'd said in a famous magazine interview that family was overrated. She still cringed when she was reminded of those words. But she'd had an excuse. Her mom had just told her that her nephew had just started kindergarten. The nephew who Julia hadn't even known existed until that little announcement. She'd been livid. But then again, it had just been an excuse. Nothing warranted speaking of family that way.

But she was repentant now. Because she was eating her words big time. Nothing on this earth was more important than family.

Julia let Wendy serve herself and then waited for Ellis to take his portion. Julia considered only taking half a chicken breast—it was more than she would've eaten had she been filming—but she reminded herself that she was retired. She could eat a whole chicken breast if she wanted to. And she really wanted it. Not only did it smell magnificent, Julia was starving. So she took the whole piece, pushing away her guilt. Some habits died hard.

"So, let's hear about the new job," Julia said as she dug into her meal with gusto. She'd not only recently rediscovered her love of family, she'd also rediscovered her long-lost love for food.

"It's good. The other tellers are pretty nice. A couple of girls cornered me and asked if you're really my aunt," Wendy said.

Julia cringed. "I'm sorry about that."

Wendy shrugged. "It was kind of informative. Living in Travers my whole life, I took for granted everyone knowing my connection to you. No one used me for it because small town gossip taught them we weren't close. And I never had to explain anything. People just knew. Now I have to explain and let people know they can't use me to get to you."

"Oh, Wendy." Julia had to deal with that kind of stuff all the time, but she didn't want her niece to have to endure the same.

"Seriously, not a big deal. Although, if you can give me a few signed photos before I leave tonight? I figure I can give those to the people who are really persistent," Wendy said with a wink.

Ellis laughed, making Julia feel better.

"And don't think you can get off scot-free," Wendy said to Ellis. "Those same girls adore you as well. They'd appreciate a signed shirtless picture."

Ellis laughed harder as Julia scowled. "He'll comply with everything but the shirtless part," she said.

Wendy smirked. "You do realize half the population of the world ogles over your boyfriend, right, Aunt Julia?"

"No, I don't. And I never will," Julia said with mock anger.

The table fell into chuckles and giggles over Julia's terrible performance.

Her phone rang, interrupting the revelry. She would've ignored it, but she saw on her watch that it was her mom.

It wasn't until Julia had the phone in her hand that she realized she could have just asked her virtual assistant to answer the call for her. She was still getting used to taking advantage of the convenience.

"Hello, Mom," Julia answered, putting her mother, Betty, on speakerphone immediately.

"Julia," Betty said in response to Julia's greeting.

"Are you calling for me or my guest?" Julia asked cheekily.

"You. But now I'm wondering if I shouldn't have bothered."

Julia knew her mom wasn't really upset. She just didn't like getting caught. And Julia knew for a fact the call was for Wendy since Betty only called Julia once a week at most, and they'd spoken the day before.

"Glad to hear from you, Mom," Julia said as a way to appease her mom's ruffled feathers.

"Hm," Betty said.

Julia bit on her lip to refrain from laughing and saw that Wendy was doing the same.

"Hi, Grandma," Wendy called out.

"Wendy." Betty said her granddaughter's name in a sweet tone Julia had never heard before. But Julia wasn't bitter about it. A grandma should have a special place in her heart for her granddaughter.

"Is Julia cooking for you?" Betty asked.

"Delicious chicken," Wendy replied.

"Is it cooked all the way through? I don't want you getting salmonella," Betty replied.

Julia couldn't be offended. She really wasn't a great cook.

"It's cooked, Grandma."

"Good," Betty replied.

Julia swore she heard a whisper on the other end before Betty asked, "And how's your new job?"

"I love it. It's been a bit of a learning curve, but every new job is like that, right? The people are nice, and a really cute guy came in and asked for my number on Friday," Wendy said.

"Wait, you didn't tell me about that," Ellis said, leaning forward in his seat.

"And I wasn't going to," Wendy retorted. "That news was for Grandma."

"I trust that you'll check into the gentleman," Betty said—it was obvious who her message was for.

"Already on it," Ellis said, his phone out.

"What did you say his name was?" Ellis asked Wendy.

"I didn't," Wendy said to Ellis before turning back to the phone. "How can you be such a traitor, Grandma?"

"If the boy was from Travers, I would have no issue. But we need to check out all these men from the big city."

Julia was about to correct her mom. Whisling was not a big city in the least. But she let it go because, compared to Travers, everywhere was a big city.

"That's fine. I'll just request security footage from the bank on Friday and then cross-check faces with the names on the transactions," Ellis said, still looking at his phone.

"You can't do that," Wendy said before biting her lip and turning to Julia. "He can't do that, can he?"

Julia shrugged. She honestly wouldn't put anything past Ellis.

"If I give you his name, you have to promise not to contact him," Wendy tried to bargain.

"I won't contact him directly," Ellis said, evading the original terms.

Wendy looked from Julia to Ellis. "Remind me never to tell the three of you anything ever again," she said with a frown. Then she said to Ellis, "It's Chad Jenkins."

"Hate that name," Ellis muttered, undeterred by Wendy's sudden bad mood.

Wendy rolled her eyes.

"I'll make sure he proceeds with caution, and we won't tell you anything unless it's life threatening," Julia promised her niece.

"Like if he's a murderer?" Wendy asked sarcastically.

"Exactly," Ellis responded with no humor.

"You do realize I'm twenty-two," Wendy said.

"You were the one who just called yourself a child," Ellis reminded.

"I should've known that would come back to bite me in the butt," Wendy muttered. But she was no longer frowning. She seemed to be taking her protective uncle in stride.

"Do you think he could be a murderer?" Betty asked.

This time Julia rolled her eyes.

"Not a chance, Mom," Julia said with confidence.

"I don't know. There on Whisling—" Betty started.

"It's just as likely to meet a murderer in Travers," Wendy interrupted. Then she grimaced as if she couldn't believe she was actually joining such a ridiculous conversation.

"Pfft," sounded from the other end of the call in a voice that was definitely not Betty's.

"Mom?" Julia asked as she and Wendy exchanged a look. They'd recognized the voice at the same time.

"Yes," Betty said, clearing her throat.

"Who's there with you?" Julia asked.

"What do you mean?" Betty answered too quickly.

"Someone else just spoke, Grandma," Wendy noted.

"Nope, just me," Betty said.

Wendy sent Julia a look that told her exactly what she wanted to do. They were going to smoke Lacey out.

"Pretty sure it wasn't you," Julia said.

"I don't know how that could be possible because I'm the only one here." Betty's voice sounded strained. As if she were sick of lying and trying to convey to someone beside her that she wanted to reveal the truth.

"Sounded a lot like my mom," Wendy said.

"Your mom?" Betty's voice reached a pitch that should've been impossible.

The line went silent. Julia imagined there was a whole lot of non-verbal communication happening on the other side. Wendy and Julia watched the phone, waiting out Betty. They could tell she was about to crack.

"Tell them," Betty whispered.

"Shh," Lacey responded.

Julia would've laughed if the situation weren't so sad. Lacey was desperate to hear from her daughter. Desperate enough to make Betty call Julia on the night Julia was having Wendy to dinner.

"This is silly, Lacey," Julia said.

"Hi, Mom," Wendy added cautiously.

"They know," Betty whispered.

"No, they don't," Lacey whispered back.

Her sister was an idiot. But Julia still loved her.

"I'd love to talk to you, Mom." Wendy offered an olive branch that her mother didn't really deserve.

"I'm not here. Tell them," Lacey whispered urgently.

"They can hear you," Betty said in a normal voice.

"No, they can't. Tell them!" Lacey demanded, her voice getting louder. She had to know the gig was up.

"Lacey, this is ridiculous. Mom, put Lacey on the phone. I'm taking it off speaker on my end," Julia said, putting the phone to her ear. She was about to say things Lacey wouldn't like, and she didn't need Wendy to hear her mother's reaction.

There was a whole lot of shuffling on the other end before Lacey said into the phone, "What."

"Good to hear your voice too, Sis," Julia said, deciding she should stop egging on her sister. For Wendy's sake.

"Is that why you had to talk to me? You needed to hear my voice?" Lacey asked.

"No," Julia said, sighing. "Lacey, I know you miss Wendy. How can you not? She is a light and a joy."

"A light and joy that would still be here if it weren't for you," Lacey said bitterly.

"I get it. You're mad at me. Maybe you hate my guts, I don't know. But don't do this again. We missed out on so much. We're still missing out on so much because of this grudge you insist on holding."

"You left us, Julia. And then you came waltzing back in and expected—" Lacey began, but Julia knew it would go on for a long time if she didn't interrupt.

"This isn't about us. This is about you and Wendy. Did you know she has her own apartment?" Julia asked. She looked up to see Ellis had drawn Wendy into conversation. Judging by Wendy's frown, it was about Chad not being good enough. But she was consumed, so she wouldn't be listening to Lacey and Julia. Thank goodness.

"She does?" Lacey asked, the marvel in her voice easy to hear.

"She already has a job and she's making friends."

"So she's moved on," Lacey said, her voice hard once more.

"No one moves on from their family," Julia replied.

"You did."

"Again, not about me. And no matter what you say about me, Wendy didn't. She misses you, Lace."

"Then she can come home," Lacey said matter-of-factly.

"Is that the only way you'll love her? If she does exactly as you ask?" Julia asked.

"Of course not."

"That's what your actions are saying."

"You're the idiot, Julia." But Lacey paused, and Julia knew her words had gotten her sister thinking.

"She has to do this. For herself. You don't have to understand, but you should support her."

"Don't tell me how to parent," Lacey snapped.

"I'm not telling you how to parent. I'm telling you how to keep from having a relationship with Wendy like the one I have with you."

That silenced Lacey.

"I'm sending you a plane ticket. Check your email in a few minutes. You don't have to take it, but you should."

"I don't need your charity—"

"This isn't for you. It's for Wendy," Julia replied. "I'll send one to mom, too. Make it a girls' trip. Come away to an island."

"Vacationing on islands has always been overrated," Lacey muttered, but Julia could tell she was wearing her down.

"Try it. And then you can tell me how much you hated it afterwards," Julia said, keeping her voice level. If she began teasing Lacey now, she'd lose her.

"I can buy my own ticket," Lacey said.

Julia grinned. She was coming.

"Then ignore the ticket I'm sending," Julia said.

Lacey huffed. "That would be a waste of money."

"It would be," Julia admitted.

"You are so stubborn. Buy the stupid ticket," Lacey said.

Julia's grin grew.

"And we wouldn't hate it if the flight was first class," Betty said from the background.

Julia pulled the phone away from her mouth so her mom and sister wouldn't hear her laugh.

"Two first class tickets coming right up. See you two soon," Julia said, turning off the phone before either woman could change her mind. She just hoped their stubbornness would keep them on this new course.

"Did you just convince my mother to visit us here?" Wendy asked, her eyes wide with amazement.

"Miracle, right?" Julia asked.

"You could say that again," Wendy replied.

Julia considered the many years she'd hoped for this very thing: family coming to visit. And now they were coming. Sure, the circumstances weren't exactly what she'd always envisioned, and it was a few dozen years later than she'd hoped, but it was happening. Miracles could be funny that way.

CHAPTER FOURTEEN

FINDING MORE service to do for Carter was a lot harder than Piper had anticipated. Sure, the picnic on the beach had been fun—a good start—but she had to do more. Yet he was the man with everything. And if he didn't have it and wanted it, he had the money and connections to acquire it immediately. Carter had friends around the world who adored him and were willing to drop anything if he needed them. Some of those friends had flown for days just to be on Whisling for Kristie's funeral. Many more had sent so many flowers that Piper's home had felt a little like a florist shop for days on end. So those kinds of things wouldn't impress Carter.

Besides, could a woman give a man flowers and chocolates or make a gesture of that sort without it being perceived as romantic? Especially if the two had a romantic past? Did a woman *ever* give a man flowers or chocolates? Piper knew she never had, but maybe she was just inconsiderate. Anyway, whatever the case, the kinds of gifts that Piper could leave on Carter's doorstep were out.

So Piper tried to remember all the things Carter had done

for her when she'd been in the midst of her grief. First and fore-most, he'd forgotten his own pain and comforted Piper. She knew she could never pay him back for that one. Her life would end before she could reciprocate what that had meant to her. Carter had been her rock. And, while Piper wished to be the same for Carter now that she wasn't such a mess, she wasn't sure how to push her way into his life enough to be his rock.

How did one become a rock? You couldn't just declare it. You had to be there for the other person. And right now, that didn't seem possible. Mostly because Piper had no idea where she stood with Carter. Honestly, even her own thoughts about the man and the role he played in her life versus the role she wanted him to play in her life were complicated. Piper loved Carter. There was no mistaking that. She had always loved him. And it seemed like the hurdles which had kept them apart were now gone. But Piper realized that she'd always wonder in the back of her mind if Carter would rather be somewhere else. How did she get over that? Anyway, needless to say, being his rock wasn't really an option.

He'd also cleaned, done and folded her laundry, mowed her lawn, basically kept Piper's life going when she couldn't. When she'd come out of her haze of grief enough to notice what he'd been doing for her, she'd been adamant that he stop. He'd insisted he had nothing better to do and that he needed to do something. Piper doubted the former but knew the latter to be true—Carter always had to be accomplishing something, and she imagined that need was only compounded by his grief—so she let it go. He'd been beyond helpful.

When she considered doing something like that for Carter, it also didn't seem like it would work. He lived in a condo so he didn't have a personal yard, and the condo association mowed the one he shared with his neighbors. Carter also had a cleaning woman come in and take care of his place, so cleaning and folding laundry were all done by a professional who probably did it much better than Piper could. She imagined interfering in that arena would only make things worse.

So what was she to do? It was then that she'd smelled her own dinner and thought maybe? She wasn't the best cook, but she knew Carter ate take-out most of the time. She could at least give him a good home-cooked meal once a week. And that's what she'd done.

Today was the second time she was taking dinner over. The first meal had gone so well that Carter had thanked her for two days straight for the simple spaghetti and meatball dinner. So Piper had decided to pull out all the stops this time, making all of Carter's favorites on one plate. She wasn't sure what she would do next week to top this, but she was going to enjoy being able to spoil her . . . daughter's father today.

Bacon wrapped meatloaf, garlic mashed potatoes, honeyed carrots, and a Caesar salad were all on the menu along with homemade onion rings as an appetizer and a chocolate trifle for dessert. Things had gotten a bit out of hand, and Piper was running late. So late that she'd texted Carter she wouldn't be able to make it to his place at the appointed hour. In true Carter fashion, he proceeded to offer to come to her.

Piper's doorbell rang.

She checked on the last batch of onion rings she had in the fryer and stirred the honeyed carrots. Both would be done soon, but she had enough time to dash to the door.

She did so, throwing it open before running back to the stove.

"It smells delectable in here," Carter said, entering the kitchen at a much slower rate than Piper had.

"Thanks," Piper said quickly as she scooped out onion rings and placed them on a paper towel to sop off the leftover oil.

Onion rings, check. The meatloaf needed to be pulled out of

the oven. Piper did that as she turned off the burner under the carrots. She then turned to the refrigerator to pull out the salad and dessert she'd stashed earlier. The mashed potatoes sat on a back burner where Piper had placed them after she'd mixed in the butter, cream, and garlic. Everything was done.

And Piper was pretty sure she only had a minimal amount of food on herself.

She looked down at the pink t-shirt and jeans she'd thrown on that morning. At least no visible food residue. She was going to call that a win.

"You made all of this?" Carter asked, looking around the kitchen.

Shoot. It was too much. Piper knew she'd bitten off more than she should chew. Carter was going to get freaked out and wonder what this gesture meant and—

She felt his warm hand wrap around her wrist.

"I see your brain going a million miles a minute. What I meant by that is this is so amazing of you," Carter said with so much meaning that Piper had to look up at him. She saw tears gathering in his eyes. Carter, the man who'd only cried at their daughter's funeral and the other very hardest moments of their journey of losing their daughter, was tearing up now?

"This means the world to me, Pipe," Carter said before clearing his throat.

"Oh, okay. So it's not too much?" Piper asked honestly.

She'd been more open and honest with Carter these past few months than in the rest of their marriage combined. They'd had to strip back so many layers while they'd been grieving together.

"It's perfect," Carter said as he let go of Piper's wrist.

She immediately missed his touch. What was going on with her? Carter was her ex. For a reason. Things needed to stay distant. Didn't they?

Yes, yes they did.

"Let me just find some to-go containers so I can wrap up your meal . . . ." Piper said as she walked toward her cupboard where she kept all her Tupperware.

"You know those onion rings will taste a whole lot better fresh," Carter said.

Piper barked out a laugh, turning back to where Carter was standing in the middle of her kitchen.

"Carter, are you angling for an invite?" Piper asked sassily.

Carter shrugged. "I figure you already have the food. Why not eat it together?"

Why not? They'd taken their meals together so many times before. First, when they'd been a couple. Then again when Kristie had gotten so sick. And, of course, there were the meals after Kristie passed when Piper had barely been able to eat. But between her parents and Carter, she'd somehow gotten enough nourishment to survive.

It seemed different now though. There'd been reasons for them to take the meals together before. What would their reason be tonight? It would be convenient—Carter was right that onion rings taste better fresh. But it was more than that. Piper could feel it. She was sure Carter knew it as well. Were they ready for this next step? To what end, Piper wasn't sure.

"I can leave if you want me to. I don't want to make this any more than you want it to be," Carter added, his voice steady yet unsure.

Why did it sound like Carter was acting as if he wanted things to be more? As if Piper was the one keeping them from moving forward? Was that the case? And if it was, did Piper want things to move forward?

She bit her lip.

"Do you mind if I grab an onion ring while you consider?" Carter asked, his eyes twinkling with mischief.

Piper laughed. He always knew how to make her do that. And Piper did want him to stay for dinner. Despite all her waffling, Piper wanted Carter there. Maybe she always had.

"Grab the plates. You know where they are," Piper said without any pomp or circumstance. This wasn't a big deal. At least it didn't have to be. Friends shared meals all the time. She wasn't sure about friends who had once been married and had a daughter together and then lost that daughter, but she was going to say that they did too. Or else she would read way too much into this.

Piper began to dish up the meal as Carter set the table. He finished his task well before Piper and lingered close as he waited for her to finish serving up his plate of food.

"All of my favorites," he said, examining Piper.

She wasn't sure what he was looking for, but she hoped he'd found it. She never wanted to be lacking in Carter's eyes.

"I figured it was the least I could do. After all you've done for me. And my therapist thought it would be a good idea," Piper added so it wouldn't feel too personal.

"You talk to your therapist about me?"

Okay, making it impersonal had backfired.

"In vague terms," Piper said, wondering what that even meant. But she'd panicked.

"What were those *vague terms?*" Carter asked.

Piper felt her cheeks flame. "Let's just eat dinner."

"Got it," Carter said with a smug smile that Piper knew all too well and yet missed incredibly. That smile had once been all hers.

Piper stared down at her meal, not appreciating the turmoil she felt every time she looked at Carter. It was too much. He was too much. What was he proposing? He was being flirty, sweet, cute, all the things he'd been while they'd been together.

He wasn't supposed to be like that toward Piper anymore. Right?

"Did I push things too far?" Carter asked.

Piper looked up from her plate and nearly laughed at how close Carter's face was. Her table seated six, but Carter had taken the chair right next to hers.

"I've been trying to be patient. I knew you needed more time," Carter said.

Piper looked at him questioningly.

"For this. For us," he said, somehow leaning in closer.

Piper didn't move. She couldn't. She was frozen by Carter's proximity but mostly by his words.

"Us?" Piper squeaked.

"You've been thinking about us, haven't you?" Carter asked.

Piper nodded, not having it in her to lie. Not when Carter was baring all.

"I've been waiting for you to see it," he said.

What was he talking about?

"See what?"

"That we're meant for each other. I know I made so many mistakes, and at first I told myself I wasn't worthy of another chance with you. I blew the greatest thing in my life: my relationship with you, our family. And I deserved every bit of misery in my heart. Then Kristie's cancer came back—"

"Whoa. Wait a second. Did you say you had regrets and *then* Kristie's cancer came back?" Piper asked, not able to wrap her mind around what Carter was saying.

Carter nodded. "I regretted leaving almost the moment after I did. But I knew I didn't deserve you back after leaving you."

"I don't get it," Piper said because what Carter was telling her went against everything she'd assumed. She thought Kristie's diagnosis had forced him home. But was he saying . . .?

"The *only* good thing to come from Kristie's relapse was that it gave me an excuse to come back to the two of you. The place I longed to be so much, it physically hurt."

Piper shook her head. She was so confused. Carter had wanted to be away. He'd needed to leave the island. He'd asked them to come with him, and Piper had said no. So he'd left. Without a backward glance. But now he was saying he'd been looking back? Longing?

"If you'd come back right away, you would have had so many regrets," Piper said, remembering all of Carter's dreams.

"Don't you know that the only regrets I harbor are the ones that have to do with leaving you and losing Kristie? Nothing else matters to me."

Piper couldn't believe what Carter was saying. He felt no pull to leave again. He wasn't here just because of a promise he'd kept to Kristie. He wanted to be here?

"I've been looking for the right moment to tell you all of this, but I'm not sure. Was this too soon?" Carter asked, meeting Piper's eyes. "I've been waiting for a long time, and I can continue to wait. Because, Pipe, I'd wait for you forever. You're it for me. You always have been. A younger, foolish me realized it a moment too late. But this me in the here and now will never do that again. I'm not sure you could ever forgive me enough to give us another chance. But if you do, I'll be here. And if you don't, I'll be here too, in whatever capacity you feel comfortable with."

Piper swallowed. She loved Carter. She always had. But all of this was so much. Sure, she'd dreamed of being with Carter again. But it had felt even less probable than Kristie visiting her again. It had been some far-off fantasy that would never come true. One that had kept her warm each night in bed all alone but drifted off when the morning light hit.

But Carter was saying it could be her reality? Their reality?

"You need some time to think," Carter said, reminding Piper

how well this man knew her. "To see if you can forgive me," he added.

Well, he was wrong there. "I forgave you long ago, Carter. How could I hold a grudge against the man who made Kristie's last couple of years so beautiful? Who held me up and then walked for me when I couldn't? And I knew you were sorry you hurt us. I just never knew you regretted leaving."

"Every moment of every day," Carter said.

"But yeah, I need time to think."

Carter smiled. "Any timeline on that thinking time?" he asked.

Piper chuckled.

"I know I don't deserve to know. But you'd be saving a wretched man a whole lot of lost sanity if you could give me anything. A month, two months . . . a year?" Carter's voice squeaked on the last word.

Piper laughed harder.

"Not a year," she promised. "I don't know where my thoughts will take me, Carter. I love you. And part of me wants to say *let's do it* right now. But that would be ignoring those niggling doubts in my mind."

"I'm fine with ignoring doubts," Carter joked. Then in a serious tone he continued, "No, I get it. I want you to face those doubts and obliterate them. I'm happy to help if I can. I want us to do this right."

"*If* we do this," Piper stated.

"Right. *If* we do this. But we'd be good together again. You have to admit that."

Piper's stomach twirled at the idea of dating Carter again. Maybe being more. But she pushed that excitement away. She needed to come at this rationally. But when had love ever been rational?

"I can wait. A whole lifetime of waiting for you is better

than any alternative without you at all," Carter said as he chomped down on an onion ring and then moaned.

"And these are divine. Kind of like you," he said with a wink that set Piper's heart fluttering.

Oh, heaven help her; she had already fallen.

CHAPTER FIFTEEN

"ELISE ISN'T MOVING," Amber said as she pushed into Nora's home. Nora was so glad to see her daughter. Last she'd seen her, Amber had been about to go for a late-night stroll. She'd called Amber that night to make sure that she'd gotten home safely, but then there'd been hardly any communication for a week. Amber had told Nora she needed time to process. Nora understood that, and she'd given Amber some space. So although Nora was always happy to see her daughter, she was a bit surprised.

Nora held her tumbler full of water—she hadn't taken the time to set it down when she'd answered the door—and watched Amber for any clue on how she should react. Amber's entire being radiated tension. So this wasn't good news. Even though this was exactly what Amber had wanted last week.

"And this is bad news?" Nora ventured to guess.

"The reason *why* she isn't moving is why I'm upset," Amber said as she threw herself onto Nora's couch. Nora took a seat next to Amber, and Amber stole her tumbler, taking a long gulp.

"Ugh. Water?" Amber asked, accusation in her gaze.

Okay. Nora needed a cheat sheet on how to deal with this

scenario. Stat. But it seemed that one wasn't going to appear anytime soon, so she said a quick prayer of guidance instead.

"I was hoping for something stronger," Amber added.

"You won't find anything stronger in any of my drinking cups," Nora said, knowing she didn't have to explain to Amber why she didn't drink. Amber hadn't been raised by Nora because of the reason why Nora no longer drank. Honestly, Amber was a big reason why Nora no longer drank.

"Oh, I know. Not like that. It's an Elise and me thing. We don't drink either, so we call soda—and on a really desperate day, juice—our strong drinks," Amber said as if she'd forgotten she was talking to Nora and not her best friend and sister.

"Ah," Nora said, realizing a little more where Amber's frustration was coming from. She was missing her closeness with Elise.

"So why isn't Elise moving?" Nora asked, needing more information if she was going to help Amber.

"It was a joint decision. Between her, Mom, and Dad," Amber said, giving Nora back her jug of water and then crossing her arms over her chest. "They're sure that now that I'm breaking up with Raul, I'll need Elise here with me."

"Oh," was all Nora said. Because the last she'd heard from Amber, calling off the wedding wasn't even a sure thing, much less breaking up with Raul. It sounded like Amber's family was assuming a lot.

"Did you talk to them?" Nora asked.

"Why should I? They've already got everything figured out. I call off the wedding. Raul breaks up with me because the only reason he would ever be with me is because I can get him a green card. Raul goes back to Argentina, and I stay here . . . needing to be comforted," Amber said, standing and throwing her arms above her as her rage grew.

"Because what they're assuming is wrong," Nora said softly,

not wanting to poke the bear. But someone had to help Amber see that communication was the only way through this.

"Does that matter to them? No. You heard that conversation with them. They talk over me or at me. I'm just so done!"

Nora digested Amber's words and then examined them, trying to say what would best help Amber and her family.

"This has happened before?" Nora asked.

"It hasn't had to. I've always followed along with their plans for me, no matter what," Amber said glumly, dropping to the couch again.

"So you haven't been living the life you've wanted?" Nora asked. That didn't seem the case to Nora, but she needed Amber to come to that realization on her own.

"I see what you're doing here," Amber said instead of answering the question.

Nora assumed Amber would. Her daughter was smart.

"Is it working?" Nora asked.

"Kind of. And I'm kind of mad at you about that," Amber said.

"Why just kind of mad?"

"Because I also know why you're doing it. And I have to admire you for that," Amber admitted glumly.

Nora worked hard not to smile. Amber was being funny, but she was far from being light-hearted.

"So?" Nora asked again.

"Yes, I've been living the life I wanted to. Because it just so happened that all of my life's decisions before this were in line with what they wanted for me. But now I've made a decision they don't like and they can't support me," Amber said.

Nora knew that was eating at her daughter. She wanted to keep a good relationship with those she loved.

"Unless . . ." Amber said, and Nora felt hopeful. Unless she communicated better with her family, right?

"Raul and I elope."

Nora dropped the tumbler she was holding, ice and water spraying across the room.

"What?" Nora asked, her eyes wide.

"I'm here to ask you to be one of our witnesses," Amber said stoically.

How had they gotten here? Nora had been sure they were on the verge of a breakthrough. This was the opposite of what Amber should be doing. It would only serve to hurt the relationships she cared so much about.

"Amber," Nora tried to keep her voice calm even as her entire soul was screaming. This was such a bad idea.

"Raul and I decided if my family can't support us, they don't need to be there on our special day. They'll only understand how important marrying Raul is to me if I go through with it. Then they'll see how wrong they were."

Nora tried to keep the incredulous look off her face. She was sure Amber would never have come to this conclusion on her own. Nora knew Amber had been conflicted when Nora had left her that evening a week before, but she would have never decided to get married without her family. That Amber from a week ago hadn't even been able to imagine planning a wedding without Elise. But somehow Amber had been convinced that she would be better off this way? Nearly family-less and friend-less on one of the most important days of her life?

"We were talking about how it would be hard not to have any family with us because Raul's family can't afford to make the trek all the way up here," Amber continued, as if she were trying to convince herself that this was only a hard solution, not an impossible one. The Amber that Nora knew would have said this scenario just couldn't happen. She couldn't get married without her family with her. And yet here she was, saying she could do it. Someone else had to be driving that decision, and that scared Nora. "But I reminded him that you can be there. You support us. So will you be there? Then at least I can have part of my family with me?"

Amber looked at Nora with such hope in her eyes, Nora knew she had to be very careful with what she said, even what she thought, at this moment. Part of her was screaming that Raul wasn't who Amber thought he was. What kind of man in love with a woman would direct her to go against her family who she absolutely adored? Why wouldn't he help her to see what Nora was trying to show Amber? That she just needed to communicate a little more.

It looked like Elise had known all along. Amber wasn't behaving like Amber. Nora was trying not to beat herself up too hard for not having seen it earlier. Although no one could've foreseen this. Amber eloping? Tabby and Elise had seemed worried that Raul was using Amber, but Nora was afraid it was even worse than that. It looked like Raul was manipulating Amber.

Nora swallowed, knowing she was Amber's last hope at staying away from this man. A man who seemed to want her to hurt the relationships that meant the most to her, isolating her. Nora had heard of these situations before, but they'd never happened in her circle and especially never to someone she loved so very much.

Desperation clawed at Nora as she tried to remain calm. What she said next could alter all of their futures, especially Amber's. She would much rather have her own happiness on the line, not Amber's.

"Amber, I really think you should talk to your family," Nora said slowly, hoping not to lose Amber.

"We went over this. They don't listen to me. They want me to do what they want me to do," Amber said.

Wait, Nora was sure they'd moved past this.

"But you wanted those things."

"I did. But now that I want something different from their grand plan for me, they can't accept me just the way I am. Because I'm not really theirs."

Nora felt a slice to her heart with those words. She couldn't imagine what that sentiment would do to Tabby and Gerry or, especially, to Elise.

"Raul pointed out to me that blood is always thicker. That's why you're standing beside me even when my family can't."

This guy was good. He knew exactly how to play on Amber's emotions and insecurities. He was even trying to play Nora through Amber's words. Thankfully, it was a lot easier to see the man's lies when one wasn't in love with him.

"I don't think Tabby and Gerry have ever thought of you as anything but theirs. You know how hard it was on your mom when I came into your life." Nora tried to point out indisputable facts.

Amber nodded, Nora's words seeming to get through to her.

"Amber, you love your family." Nora had to send her point home. Push away all the doubts Raul had planted.

"I do. And I know they love me. But that love isn't enough for them to just accept me for me," Amber said.

No, they love you so much they don't want you to make the biggest mistake of your life Nora almost said but held her tongue.

"Once we're married, they'll see how wrong they were and they'll come around," Amber said decisively.

What Amber said made sense and didn't all at once.

"They'll be so hurt," Nora said.

"Like I am now. Elise is laughing with the employees. Acting like life is just fine and dandy. She doesn't see what she's done. How much she's hurt me. But I'm getting over it. They will too."

And Raul will have what he wants. Amber married to him

while her relationships have suffered so much that she'll have him and only him. What would he do then? Make Amber choose her family or him? Suddenly Nora thought of another reason why Raul would be manipulating Amber like this. Amber was so much more than a green card. She was a meal ticket. She owned half of a flourishing company.

"You'll sign a prenup, right?" Nora asked suddenly before gauging her words.

"You sound like them now," Amber said lightly before really looking at Nora. "That was a joke, right?"

She wasn't going to make Raul sign a prenup either. Nora didn't know how this could get any worse. She'd never even thought of any of this before because Amber herself was such a catch. Why would anyone use and manipulate her? But she also saw how her kindhearted daughter was just the type of woman a man like Raul would target. She loved so hard. And Raul was using that love against her. Nora tried to bite back the hatred she felt building for Raul.

"Not a joke. It could be a good idea. Raul has his own assets he'd like to protect as well, right?" Nora asked.

"But nothing he wouldn't want to share with his wife. Mama Nora, Raul and I have to be all in or we're putting ourselves at a disadvantage from day one. If we want this to work, we have to give it our all. Be willing to give up everything," Amber said.

Yes, Amber had to be willing to give up her family and her company while Raul gave up what? His fears that he'd never be a US citizen? It was easy to see those words had been fed to Amber by Raul.

But Raul was right about one thing. Marriage should be all in. Even if he was just using those words as manipulation.

So Nora agreed with Amber. "You're right. I'm sorry. But marriage should also be a family affair, right?" Nora asked.

"Not if my family is against it."

"They didn't say they were against it though. They just wanted you to take some more time."

"And they assumed we'd break up," Amber said. "Because they doubt Raul's love for me."

Nora felt sick because she could feel Amber's love for Raul but distrusted that it was truly reciprocated.

But wait, it *had* seemed like Raul loved Amber. At least when Nora saw them interact together. Granted, Raul could be a great actor but . . . Nora took a deep breath. She felt how tightly she was wound up and needed to relax. She'd make no good decisions from this place of anxiety and fear. She needed a clear mind and an even clearer heart.

As she pushed fear from her mind, a whole new thought entered. What if Nora was wrong? Sure, all that she'd heard could easily be interpreted the way she had, but maybe Raul wasn't the villain in all of this. Nora hardly knew the man; she was judging him based on Amber's actions and her own fears. She'd judged Raul hastily. They all had. Because they hadn't had time to do anything else. But maybe they'd all come to the wrong conclusion. That tiny hope radiated brightly. Maybe Raul wasn't manipulating Amber but was hurting for her and reacting in all the wrong ways? Raul hardly knew Amber's family, and the family hardly knew Raul. What they all needed was time. But that was a commodity Amber was sure they had way too little of. So Nora had to try to fight for more of it. For all their sakes.

"They don't know him. Honestly, I don't know him. And Raul doesn't know them. But I do know you, Amber. You want us all to love Raul the way you do. I think we just need more time."

That last line could've been a lie. If Raul turned out to be the manipulating man Nora had pegged him to be, no amount of time would be enough for her to approve of him. But she was willing to lie right now if it meant protecting her baby. Or she was wrong and Amber didn't need protecting because Raul loved her as much as he claimed to. But Nora wanted to see either scenario play out well before a wedding.

"We don't have time," Amber retorted.

Nora practically saw thoughts of an expiring visa swimming through Amber's head.

"I know. But you weren't planning on getting married until November anyway. We still have two months. Give us at least a family get together. A weekend in Seattle, just the six of us."

Amber pursed her lips, seeming to mull over the situation.

"What about Bobby and Mack?" Amber asked about her birth father and Nora's boyfriend.

It would be wonderful to have Mack with her, but Nora was worried about adding Bobby to the mix. He tended to stir things up. And that was the last thing they needed right now. But it wouldn't be fair to include Mack and not Bobby. So Nora was willing to sacrifice having Mack with her in order to keep Bobby away as well. She said the first excuse she could come up with. "You know how crazy Bobby's work schedule is, and you know how Bobby would feel if Mack is with us and he isn't."

Amber nodded.

"I won't make you talk to your parents or do anything you don't feel comfortable with. I do think you should talk to your parents, but that's up to you. No pressure on anything. You get to show off that handsome fiancé of yours, and he gets to know the people who mean the most to you. If you haven't won everyone over by the end of the weekend, at least you'll have that memory when things get hard right after the elopement."

Amber nodded slowly, seeming to consider all aspects.

"And you won't say anything to my parents?"

Nora shook her head. "We can say that Raul took news about the postponed wedding well. He wants to get to know your family before he goes back to Argentina since you'll probably get married while he's still in Argentina." Another lie. But Nora would keep saying them if they got them all to this weekend getaway. She hoped some miraculous solution to what she should do would come before then. Or maybe Raul would prove them all wrong. Oh how she wished that to be the case.

"And if it doesn't work?" Amber asked.

"Then we elope," Nora said, her biggest lie of all. As long as Nora was here on this earth, there was no way in heck Amber was eloping with Raul. Either they'd all see they were wrong about him over this getaway and Amber would get the big family wedding she'd always dreamed of or Raul would be exposed.

CHAPTER SIXTEEN

THE WEATHER WASN'T GREAT. Alexis tried to breathe in and out, but the clouds felt like a bad omen.

She'd done what she was supposed to and waited the one month that Marsha had asked. Alexis had even refrained from seeing Jared. Because if they were going to do this, they wanted to really do this. In full view of the kids. With the kids' full support. And that meant Alexis spending time with the kids before going back to dating Jared completely.

But now she was second guessing that decision like no other. Was it really so bad to date in secret?

She knew that it was. Especially with a man like Jared. She wanted to shout that he was hers from the rooftops and never ever hurt his children in the process.

But doing this the right way meant opening herself up to the scrutiny of Jared's two precious children once more. Children who had done a pretty good job of letting Alexis know they did not like her. Granted, it had been thanks to their mother that they had seen Alexis as a homewrecker. Now that Marsha had stopped feeding the kids lies, would they stop hating Alexis?

Jared was hopeful. Oh, sweet Jared. Alexis couldn't help but smile when she thought about how hard he'd worked in the interim. He had also respected Marsha's one month rule, and although he'd missed Alexis like crazy, he'd actually kind of appreciated it because it had given him time to sing Alexis's praises before she was back in their lives.

But today was the day. A few days over a month later because it was Jared's first day off since the one month mark had passed.

The four of them, just the four of them, were going into Seattle to spend the day together at a waterpark. Jared had assured Alexis that this was an activity both of his children loved, and it would be even more special because it was one of the very last days the park would be open this year. It was also perfect because they'd have time on the ferry and in the car to be together, but then they'd have their own space at the waterpark.

It all made sense. In Alexis's head, they'd done everything they could. So how could this not go well? She'd heard from her mother that Peter and Brittany were less closed off than they'd been before their mother's accident. Back when Marsha had been warning them that Margie would try to take the place of their late grandmother. They were warmer with Bill and even with Margie. It hurt Alexis's heart that those poor kids had been scared for so long, all because their mother had lied to them. Fury began to grow, but Alexis tried to brush it away. Anger towards Marsha would help no one. Sure, the woman wasn't willing to help Alexis, but Alexis would never expect that from her boyfriend's ex. As long as she kept her word and really didn't hinder things, Alexis would be more than happy.

But therein lay a little of Alexis's trepidation. The kids had stayed with Marsha last night. Jared would be picking them up and then coming straight to Alexis's. So what if Marsha had gone back on her word at the last minute? What if the kids had once again been poisoned to the idea of Jared having a relationship with Alexis?

Because when it came down to it, Alexis didn't trust Marsha. She wasn't sure she ever would. She might be able to fully forgive her one day, but trusting her? That felt like too much. So until she saw with her own two eyes that those adorable children hadn't again been indoctrinated by their mother, Alexis wasn't going to allow herself to hope wholeheartedly.

Part of her wondered if today would end like the other days when she'd attempted to have a relationship with the two people that mattered most to the man who mattered most to her. Would she be crying her eyes out in just a few hours?

The sound of Jared's car pulling into her driveway hit Alexis's ears. She looked down at the bags she was holding, ready for his arrival. The first bag held towels, a change of clothes, sunscreen, and anything else one might need at a waterpark. The second was a cooler bag full of the kids' favorite foods. Alexis had one true talent, cooking, and she wasn't above bribing anyone with her talent.

Knocking came from the front door and she drew in a deep breath. This was it. She looked over her reflection in the full-length mirror in her entryway and saw what she expected to see. A yellow sundress covering a black tankini along with a terrified face. She really needed to change her expression before she opened the door. Alexis practiced a smile in the mirror that looked a lot more constipated than happy. Oh man, what was she going to do? She burst out a single laugh and the look on her face was okay. She still looked a little like she might throw up, but she no longer looked like she'd missed her morning constitutional. It would have to do.

"Everything okay in there?" Jared called out.

He must have heard Alexis's weird laugh. He also had to

know that this day would be wreaking havoc on her nerves. She'd lived these past months without Jared. She knew she could survive, but she didn't want to just survive life. To be so close to having him back and then to maybe lose him again? It would be too much. Alexis wondered if it was safer to just stay in her home and hide behind her couch.

She concluded that it was definitely safer, but Jared was worth a whole new heartbreak. Even just imagining it made her heart sink, but she could do this. For Jared, for herself, and even for those kids. They hadn't wanted Alexis in their lives, but she knew that if they let her in, she could be someone they could rely on. Another person to love them. And everyone needed more people to love them, right?

"Alexis?" Jared called out, worry tinging her name.

"I'm fine. I'm right—" Alexis opened her door and he took her breath away. It had been far too many days since Alexis had last seen his face. Somehow the love she had for him grew in that moment. She dropped her bags and flung herself into his arms.

Jared caught her and held her close, breathing in her scent. She wanted nothing more than to reach her lips up to his but decided that would probably scar the poor kids in the car before they even started the day. So she refrained and instead pressed a kiss to Jared's chest. The kids wouldn't be able to see that.

"I missed you." Alexis said the words that felt far too tame for what she felt.

Jared nodded as he continued to hold Alexis to him. "So much," he added.

As much as she didn't want to do it, Alexis began to pull away. She needed to get to the car. Get to know the kids better without the wall of Marsha obstructing any chance at a relationship between them.

"Not yet," Jared whispered as he kissed the top of her head and ran his hand up and down her back.

"Your kids," Alexis reminded, trying to look around him to see how the kids were taking their reunion.

"Can wait. It's their fault I haven't seen you for this long."

"Marsha's fault," Alexis amended.

"Yeah, yeah. I know. I'm not actually mad at them for anything, but I am willing to use them as an excuse to keep you in my arms for as long as possible."

Alexis laughed against Jared's chest. She was against Jared's chest again. She could hardly believe it. She wanted to let her hands roam along his back the way he was doing to her, but her hands were in full view of the kids, so she didn't. She was going to be on her best behavior. And then, hopefully, she would be rewarded with the make out session of a lifetime . . . after she'd won the kids over and they were in bed for the night.

"Dad!" Peter yelled from the car.

This time Jared put up less resistance as Alexis pushed away. She was out of his arms, her body feeling cold. She didn't like it, but it needed to be done.

She leaned over to grab her bags but Jared beat her to it. He took both of them, waiting patiently as Alexis closed and locked her front door.

This was it. Her heart beat against her ribcage as she walked toward Jared's car. She was sure that she would know just by the looks on their faces if anything had changed. Alexis had to be brave and meet those gazes.

She lifted her eyes and noticed that Brittany was on the side of the car nearest to her. Alexis shot her a smile and then remembered how she'd looked in the mirror. In order to go back to the non-constipated smile, she barked out a single very loud laugh, causing Jared to turn and look at her. Even Peter leaned over to Brittany's side of the car, a confused expression on his face. Jared shot her a concerned smile. She could hear him asking if she was okay, and she would be . . . just as soon as she died from embarrassment and came back to earth in a new body. Hey, maybe Jared's kids would like her better then?

Alexis gave Jared a tiny nod and then turned her attention back to Brittany. But the girl was now turned toward Peter, the two of them talking about something. Probably about how weird their dad's girlfriend was.

Alexis was about to get in the car and she still had no idea where she stood with the kids. Jared opened her door and then went to the trunk to put her bags in it. She realized she had a few moments with just the kids. It was time to stop being a mess and make this work. This was her chance with Jared. She was not going to blow it. She was going to knock these kids' socks off. Sure, they hadn't liked her in the past, but they'd never given her a chance. And now she hoped they would. This was going to work. It had to work.

So Alexis turned in her seat to meet the kids head-on. The glares, which had been the only looks Brittany and Peter had given to Alexis in the past, were missing. There were no smiles in their places, but Alexis would take these curious stares over glares any day. At least the kids seemed open to her. That was more than she would've dared to hope for a month before. Now she'd spend the day winning them over.

"You guys excited for the waterpark?" Alexis asked lamely, realizing she should've come up with conversation points before today. What had she been thinking? What did middle school kids care about these days?

"Yeah," Peter said while Brittany shrugged.

Shoot, a shrug wasn't a good thing. Brittany had shrugged plenty for past Alexis. They were supposed to have moved beyond the shrug.

"What's your favorite slide?" Alexis asked, turning to the front of the car. Memories of her own teen years filled her head.

She would've hated any adult who seemed like she was trying too hard. And, oh boy, was Alexis trying too hard.

She needed to chill out. *Chillax* as the kids said. Wait, did the kids say *chillax* anymore? She really should've done some research. Maybe watched a few hours of teen influencers on YouTube.

But she was here now. And her best plan thus far was chilling out. So she was going to do just that. While not saying *chillax*.

Peter went on to explain the tallest slide in the park. It had a cover right at the top so people wouldn't fly off of it, and then it went down at nearly a ninety-degree angle for the rest of the slide. That sounded terrifying to Alexis, but she didn't voice her fears. Instead, she told Peter that sounded amazing.

"So you'll ride it with me?" he asked. "Dad and Brittany get too scared."

"I don't get scared, per se," Jared said, getting into the car and turning to Peter. "I'm trying to impress this girl," he whispered, but the whole car heard.

"Pretty sure she's already impressed," Brittany said. Alexis wanted to turn around to see her face, but that wouldn't be chillaxing. Had Brittany been upset as she'd spoken? Alexis had been able to tell so little by Brittany's tone.

"So will you?" Peter asked.

"You don't have to," Jared reassured Alexis with a pat on her knee.

But she was pretty sure she did. Even if she might fall to her death. At least it would be for a good cause.

"Sure," Alexis said as her hands went clammy.

"Yes!" Peter said as Brittany asked, "Seriously?"

Again, Alexis could tell so little from Brittany's tone, but at least it seemed like she'd begun to win over one of Jared's kids. All it took was risking her life.

Before Alexis knew it, they'd ridden the ferry, traversed Seattle freeways and arrived at the waterpark . . . and she still had no idea what Brittany thought of her. Brittany had spoken a few times during the car ride. She'd responded every time she'd been spoken to, even when Alexis had asked her questions. But her tone was reserved, almost as if she was waiting for something. Alexis had no idea what or if that something could come along, but she sure hoped it would.

"There it is," Peter said, pointing up to a gigantic slide that Alexis could see, even from the parking lot of the waterpark.

This was it. The way she was going to go. She was going to die at this waterpark trying to win the approval of Jared's children.

Screams came from within, and Alexis knew she'd made a grave error. But she was here. Nothing short of a miracle would save her now.

Jared held her hand as they walked into the waterpark. He could sense Alexis's tension.

"You really don't have to go on that ride," Jared whispered when Peter's attention was turned to the slides.

"I know. But I want to," Alexis whispered back. It was then she noticed that Brittany had been watching them closely. As soon as Alexis caught her eye, Brittany turned away.

Alexis had a feeling Brittany was judging her and really wished the girl would hold up some score cards or something. At least that way she would know where she stood. If only life could be so easy.

"Let's go," Peter said to Alexis as soon as his dad had paid for their tickets.

"Hold your horses," Jared interjected. "Let's find some open chairs and have a meeting spot set up before you go running off."

That sounded like a great idea to Alexis. Anything to put off riding the slide.

Jared leisurely took in his surroundings before leading the group toward some open chairs. Peter anticipated his move, running ahead to the chairs and throwing his t-shirt on one before running back to Alexis.

"Let's do this!" he said, jumping to amp himself up for the ride.

Alexis nodded, peeling off her sundress and throwing it the way Peter had. She could totally do this.

Plus, it was so cute to see Peter like this. Alexis knew that fourteen was a rough age. It was a time of feeling grown up with many of the instincts of a child. And it wasn't often that the childlike side of Peter came out. She'd do anything to fuel that youthful enthusiasm. Even plunge to her death.

She jumped up and down a few times like Peter had and then followed him to the line that led to the gigantic slide.

They wound up a few flights of stairs and were getting near the top when Alexis made the mistake of looking over the edge.

Her knees went weak and her hands got sweaty. She totally could not do this.

She glanced up to see only five kids in front of Peter and then a line of about twelve teens behind her. Not a single adult was among them. Because all the adults knew better. Except for Alexis.

"Make sure to keep your legs crossed," Peter said, still thrilled. He seemed to completely miss that Alexis was about to die of fear before even reaching the slide.

"Legs crossed. Got it," Alexis somehow managed to respond.

"Do you have a hair tie?" a girl behind Alexis asked.

Alexis nodded, raising her wrist.

"You might want to put your hair up. This slide can mess it up pretty bad," the girl advised.

Alexis nodded again. The closer she got to the top of the slide, the less her tongue seemed to work.

She put her hair up in a messy bun, avoiding looking down at the ground at all costs.

There were now only two kids in front of Peter.

Au revoir, life, Alexis thought. She'd had a good run. It looked like no miracle would be forthcoming. She was going to have to go down this slide.

"It's Dad and Brittany," Peter said, pointing down.

Alexis knew she had to look over the edge whether she wanted to or not. She drew up the courage and took a step closer so that she could see where Peter was pointing. Sure enough, there stood Jared waving up at them and Brittany watching.

Alexis gave Jared a small wave, all she could manage considering how little her body parts were obeying her.

She swore she saw Jared mouth something, but there was no way she could read his lips at that distance. It felt like it was nearly a mile down. Alexis knew that wasn't the case, but reality wasn't something she had a complete hold on at the moment.

"You can go," the teen at the top of the slide told Peter.

He hopped into the plastic tube and gave Alexis a thumbs up. "See ya down there," he said happily. "And don't forget to cross your legs," he called as he fell out of sight.

Oh my gosh. That was going to be Alexis. She waited for a scream, any sign to show that Peter had made it down safely, but she heard nothing.

"Okay, you're up," the teen said, looking at Alexis.

Oh. He was talking to her. She was up. Peter had made it.

Alexis looked at the stairs behind her. She could always walk back down. Peter had already had her company all the way up. It hurt no one but her pride for her to turn around.

And yet she couldn't. It felt like she was breaking her word to even consider it.

"Ma'am?" the teenaged worker asked.

Right. She had to get on and push herself off. Then plunge down to the bottom, a mile below.

Her shaky hands cried for her to take the stairs, but Alexis wouldn't do it.

Before her rational side could get in the way, Alexis sat, feeling the water rushing around her.

Could she do this?

She had to.

She lay down and pushed off, sailing forward for a moment before plunging. Screams escaped her that she didn't know she was capable of as she sailed down the slide, her back actually lifting off the plastic at a moment in time before she finally reached the safety of the bottom of the slide.

She'd done it. She'd survived.

Alexis lay there a moment, letting the water rush over her head. She'd done it.

She opened her eyes to see Jared, a gigantic smile on his face as he reached out a hand toward her.

Alexis accepted the hand and let him pull her off the slide and into a hug.

"I can't believe you did it," Peter said. "I totally thought you were going to take the stairs back down like dad did the time he said he would ride this ride with me."

Alexis shot an accusing look up at Jared. He'd backed down? But Alexis figured he didn't have anything to prove to his own kids.

"Not helping my game, Son," Jared said to Peter before nodding down at Alexis, still shivering in his arms. Alexis had no idea why she was shivering but loved the feeling of doing so in Jared's arms.

"Like you have game, Dad," Peter said with a laugh as he turned away. "I'm going to go in the lazy river," he said as he began walking away.

"Thanks for coming with me, Alexis," Peter called over his shoulder as if it were nothing. But those words meant everything to Alexis.

She smiled and then pulled away from Jared. She had yet to see Brittany since she'd come off the slide. Had her death-defying stunt impressed the unimpressible?

"Dad, can I talk to Alexis for a minute?" Brittany asked, coming up from behind Jared and causing him to take a step back from Alexis.

He sent Alexis a look that said he'd do as she wanted, so Alexis nodded once. She wanted exactly this.

"I guess I'll catch up to Peter in the lazy river," Jared said, walking backwards for a few steps and making sure all was well.

Alexis nodded again as Brittany said, "Go Dad!" shooing him with her hands.

When Jared finally jumped into the lazy river, Brittany turned back to Alexis before looking up at the top of the slide.

"How scary was that?" Brittany asked.

"Honestly? Terrifying," Alexis said as she gazed up with Brittany. She'd just come down from there. On a piece of plastic.

"Why did you do it?" Brittany asked, still looking up at the slide to watch as the next teen flew down.

Alexis had a feeling this was some sort of test. She desperately wanted to pass it, but she had to be completely honest.

"Because Peter wanted me to," Alexis replied.

"And you want to impress us?" Brittany asked, still not meeting Alexis's eye.

This was definitely a test. So Alexis answered the next question as carefully as she could. "At first it was just that. And I guess I didn't want to let Peter down. He seemed so excited about the slide."

"But then?" Brittany prodded, now looking at Alexis.

"I thought about walking back down when I was up there. But I knew what that would say if I did. I don't know you and Peter well, but I wanted you guys to know that I'd have your backs if you ever needed me. It felt like Peter needed me. So I had his back."

Brittany bit her lip as she turned her head to examine Alexis. What was she looking for?

"Would you do it again? With me?" Brittany asked.

Alexis nodded without hesitation. She'd be terrified once more, but she would do anything to show Brittany she was on her side.

"Why?" Brittany asked. "Is it less scary now?"

"Oh hell no. Way scarier now that I've done it. But I have your back," Alexis said.

"Does that mean you'll do anything I ask?" Brittany asked.

Alexis chuckled. "Nice try. Not anything. But everything that doesn't go against your dad's wishes for you, I would do my best."

"Like finding those shoes?"

Alexis had almost forgotten about that outing because it had felt like such a failure. She'd been sure she'd made a breakthrough, only for Brittany to seem to hate her more the next time she saw her.

"Yeah."

"That was pretty cool of you," Brittany said.

"We needed those shoes," Alexis replied.

Brittany smiled. The full blown one that Alexis had only ever seen her offer her father. She was giving one to Alexis.

Tears pricked Alexis's eyes. She blinked them back, knowing Brittany would hate it if Alexis started blubbering all over her.

"Yeah. The girls at school thought they were awesome."

"I'm glad."

Alexis stood, unsure of what to do next. Did that smile mean she'd passed the test?

"I guess we should go find Dad and Peter?" Brittany asked Alexis. She had asked Alexis her opinion. Alexis was going to write this moment down in her journal with her favorite pen.

"Sounds good," Alexis said as she walked side by side with Brittany toward the lazy river.

Alexis hadn't gotten her miracle to save her from the slide, but she realized if she'd gotten that one, she would've missed out on this one. And she wouldn't trade the miracle of Brittany giving her a chance for the world.

Now she had to try not to blow it.

CHAPTER SEVENTEEN

THE AIR WAS GETTING CRISP, telling Julia the holidays were nearly upon them. She loved this time of year as it brought the anticipation of gatherings and joy still to come.

She closed the door after her latest guest, one of Wendy's friends from work, entered. Julia glanced around the room at the people she called friends. She couldn't believe that just a year before, she had been the one to be a guest of honor at one of these house parties. Now she was hosting one for Wendy. Julia felt completely at home with these people who had become like family. What a difference a year could make.

She glanced over at her living room to see a lively conversation between Bess, Dax, Lily, Allen, Deb, and Luke. She'd invited Nora to the party as well, but Nora had called a few days later to say that she was so sorry to decline but Amber's parents would be coming into town the same weekend. Julia had said that everyone should come along—Wendy would probably appreciate having Amber and Elise attend since they were closer in age to her—but Nora had said they were all going away together and would be in Seattle for the weekend. When Julia had told Deb she hoped her sister was having a good time in

Seattle, Deb had given Julia a weird smile. One that made Julia wonder if there wasn't more going on with Nora than she'd first assumed.

But she was sure Nora would work it out. She always seemed to, even when life threw rock-hard lemons at her.

"Missing me?" Ellis asked as he came up behind Julia and wrapped his arms lovingly around her waist.

"Always," Julia said as she turned to give Ellis a quick peck and then pulled out of his arms. She knew if she hung out in them for too long, she'd give her guests a show they hadn't paid for.

"Please tell me you aren't still nervous," Ellis said when Julia tugged away from him.

Julia bit her lip. Nervous? Oh right. She'd almost forgotten that her mom and sister were coming into town in just a couple of weeks. She drew in a deep breath. She was excited. She really was. Especially for Wendy. It would mean the world to her to show her mom and grandma her new life here. But Julia couldn't help but feel some trepidation. Would her family judge her life and find it lacking? Find her lacking? Probably. But Ellis had pointed out that what her family thought wasn't up to Julia. All Julia could control was her reaction to them. And she was doing her best to remember that. She didn't have an issue with anyone else judging her—she'd gotten used to that over her years of living in the limelight—but family was always different. For better or worse.

"Not really. Not with you around. But I knew if I stayed in your arms, I wouldn't be able to stop at just a peck," Julia said with a mischievous grin.

"And what would be wrong with that?" Ellis drawled, warming Julia to her core.

"Our guests." Julia nodded toward the groups of people gathered in her home.

"I think they just wore out their welcome," Ellis replied, looking ready to clear the room.

Julia laughed. The party had barely started.

"Fine. But when you're ready to kick these people out, you know where to find me, Darlin'," Ellis added, causing Julia to laugh harder.

Dang, she loved that man.

Julia's loud laughter caused the group conversing near her to look over their way.

"Hey Ellis, how's that new album coming along?" Luke asked Ellis, drawing him into their conversation.

Ellis walked a few steps toward their friends before turning back and winking at Julia. She grinned like the lovesick fool she was.

Julia wanted to follow him, but she decided that as hostess, she really should check on the rest of their guests. Besides, she already knew the answer to Luke's question. Ellis's album was nearing completion and his record company was urging him strongly to get a tour set up. Julia knew he had to do it—it was his job—but she was dreading the day Ellis left her behind for months on end.

But those were worries for another day. Today was about celebrating her sweet niece moving to Whisling.

Judging by the laughing crowd enveloping Wendy, she was acclimating just fine. Julia passed right on by that group, knowing she was probably too old for whatever they were conversing about. She didn't want to be the overeager aunt trying to butt into things when she wasn't needed or wanted. She'd hang out with Wendy later.

"How are you all doing?" Julia interrupted a conversation between Alexis, Jared, and Lou.

"I'm just trying to figure out who you got to cater this little shindig since it wasn't me or Bess," Alexis said with a puffed pastry in hand. It didn't look like she was going to eat it any time soon. She appeared to be looking for clues.

Julia laughed. "You can't figure it out?" she asked.

Alexis shook her head. "I mean, the food isn't bad. But it's not mine either."

Julia laughed harder. Her friend had no shame when it came to bragging about her cooking.

"What she means to say is *thank you for inviting us. We're grateful for your gracious offer,*" Lou said, shooting her best friend a glare.

"She's fine. I knew the food wouldn't be amazing. We had Ellis's cook whip together what she could, and then she helped us warm up some ready-made stuff from the grocery store."

Alexis gasped.

"I wanted you and Bess to feel like guests, not hired help," Julia said, defending her decision.

"Don't," Alexis replied quickly.

"Let you feel like a guest?" Jared asked, a chuckle following his words.

"Exactly. Next time let me cook," Alexis demanded.

The group laughed.

"Will do," Julia promised.

"We all know Alexis's need to show off her cooking skills," Lou teased.

"When you got it, flaunt it. Kind of like you're doing with those brand-new guns," Alexis returned with a grin as she pointed to Lou's exposed arms, thanks to the tank top she wore. They were looking rather toned.

The teasing continued, and Julia watched rather than listened to the group.

Lou was beaming. In the last month or so, Julia had noticed a change in her friend's countenance. Sure, she seemed a bit more fit, but it was more than that. She just seemed at peace.

Julia wondered if Lou's ex finally moving in with his new girl-friend had helped that along. Sometimes the only way to truly get over someone was to see them moving forward. It looked like Lou was now doing so as well, and Julia couldn't be more pleased for her

If Lou was beaming, Alexis was shining like a diamond. Ever since she and Jared had made it official again, Julia hadn't seen anything but a smile on Alexis's face. Even while she'd been scolding Julia about not using her services, she'd been smiling. And Julia didn't blame her. Alexis had finally gotten the man of her dreams and a family to boot. It sounded like there was still some work to do in winning Jared's kids all the way over, but they seemed to be starting to accept Alexis. That was definitely a step in the right direction.

"Julia," Gen called, and Julia turned to see another of her glowing friends. Gen had just announced a second pregnancy, a third child for them, and although she'd told Julia that she and Levi were overwhelmed by the thought of three children, they were also thrilled.

Julia walked over to where Gen was speaking to Piper. She'd seen Piper walk in on the arm of her ex-husband, Carter. She'd been surprised but kept her questions to herself. Julia was the last to judge where love grew. She just knew it should be cherished once it blossomed.

"I wanted to show Piper your color," Gen said, combing through Julia's locks as Julia came to Gen's side.

That was a hazard of being friends with your hairdresser. You never knew when your hair would be put on display.

"Oh, I love it," Piper said as she gazed at the blonde on Julia's head. Julia changed her hair color frequently. She could only do so because Gen was very good at what she did. Julia had gone dark right after leaving Hollywood but then decided she liked being light for summer and darker for winter. Right now she still had her summer color in, even though it was already October. But she was seeing Gen next week and would be going dark again.

"This after over a month of growth?" Gen asked.

Julia nodded.

"Wow, it grows out beautifully," Piper gushed.

"Oh stop it," Julia and Gen responded in unison.

All three women laughed.

"So you could come in and we could do something like this," Gen said, showing Julia just how much the woman was itching to get her hands on Piper's hair.

Piper had a gorgeous natural light brown color, but Julia could see how a few blonde highlights would liven it up. Julia was guessing Piper hadn't thought much about her appearance in the last year or more between Kristie's illness and then her death.

Julia's stomach clenched at just the thought of losing a child. Even though Julia wasn't a mother, she could still imagine the heartache that would follow maybe the most terrible of losses. But even as Julia thought that, she realized there should be no comparing of grief. Grief was grief. Loss was loss. In the moment one was experiencing it, it felt like the worst pain imaginable.

But Piper seemed to be weathering the loss so much better these days. Time might not heal wounds, but it did give people the ability to learn how to survive and then thrive through the pain.

"So what's up with you and Carter?" Gen asked the question Julia would've never dared to. Granted, Gen had known Piper a whole lot longer than Julia had since the two had both grown up on the island.

Piper blushed beautifully before glancing behind Julia. Julia knew Carter was standing a few feet behind her at the buffet.

"I don't know," Piper said as she smiled.

"But something good," Gen concluded.

"I guess you could say that. We're friends. He's been exactly who I've needed."

"I'd say you're more than friends," Gen teased.

"No, we're just friends," Piper replied adamantly.

"For now," Gen said with a pump of her eyebrows, and Piper didn't disagree. The two then fell into conversation about people Julia didn't know, so she backed away from the conversation once again, scanning the crowd of people she'd grown to care about and thinking about what they'd gone through, what they were overcoming.

She remembered the words of Alexis earlier that week. She'd told Julia that Jared's kids starting to accept her was nothing short of a miracle. Julia had felt the same way about her sister being willing to visit, and Piper's healing was also a miracle in its own right.

Julia realized that those beautiful moments when earth and the beyond harmonized weren't as uncommon as she'd once assumed. Julia could name quite a few miracles that she'd experienced in the past few years, things coming together just right for the good of herself and those around her.

Sometimes the miracles were big, sometimes they were small, but they were incredible regardless. And when one had hope for miracles, life could never be very bleak. Living on Whisling Island had taught her that.

Made in the USA
Monee, IL
03 January 2022